D1525410

A PERFECT CHRISTMAS SURPRISE

KRINGLE, TEXAS BOOK 3

LORI WILDE

CHAPTER 1

RANCHER CALEB SUTTON walked into the vet clinic, intent on picking up six dogs for his neighbors, Marjorie and Ted Miller.

The Millers ran Kringle Kritters Rescue which butted up against the backside of his property, the Leaping Longhorn Ranch. They had dropped the rescued animals off that morning for their vaccinations.

Ted had a doctor's appointment in Fort Worth and they'd asked Caleb if he'd mind bringing the dogs back after they'd received their shots.

He hadn't minded. This was Kringle, Texas, where people looked out for each other, but glancing around at the chaotic scene, Caleb had a powerful urge to skedaddle.

Dogs barked. Cats meowed. A parrot kept squawking out "Merry Christmas!" Kids chased each other around while holiday carols blared. Wall-to-wall animals packed the facility, all controlled by their owners with varying degrees of success.

Dang, but he disliked surprises. Why hadn't the Millers warned him something was afoot at the clinic?

After a nomadic childhood as a military brat, his father's career moving them from pillar to post with dizzying frequency, he'd come to crave security, serenity, and stability. Pandemonium threw him for a loop, and it was all he could do not to bolt for the door.

What in the blue blazes was going on around here?

At the back of the room stood his good friend and rancher, Zach Delaney. Zach was dressed as Santa, fake beard and all.

Zach waved jovially. "Hey, there, Caleb, welcome to the madhouse. Ho, ho, ho!"

Yikes. His friend was such a good sport. You wouldn't catch Caleb wearing a Santa getup. No way, no how, no siree.

Caleb strolled farther into the clinic, his eyes

widening to take in the full scope of the hubbub. "What's all this?"

"Pictures with Santa," called a cheery feminine voice behind him.

Caleb froze.

The pulse at his throat ticked hot and fast. He didn't have to turn around to know who'd spoken. He'd once been engaged to that voice and she'd turned his life upside down.

"Could you please scooch over a bit, cowboy? You're blocking the shot."

Caleb swiveled to see Ted and Marjorie's daughter, Ava Miller, standing behind a camera tripod dressed in a crazy candy cane costume. She gave him her patented, sunshine-infused smile.

Once upon a time, that brilliant, unwavering smile had been his kryptonite. *Once upon a time?* The way his pulse pounded hard against his veins it still was.

Double dang.

Caleb curled his fingers into fists. How had he not seen Ava when he'd first stepped into the room?

The candy cane suit. That was how. It hid her gorgeous body and cloaked her beautiful hair.

The illogical way his stomach jumped, and his

chest heated, startled him. *Thanks so much for the heads-up, Ted and Marjorie.*

Was this some kind of setup? Were his neighbors playing matchmaker? He hoped not. Why would they? It had been ten years since he and their daughter had been high school sweethearts too quickly on the road to matrimony.

"Cabe," Ava said, calling him by the nickname only she'd ever used. She made a little shooing motion with her hand and deepened the hue of her smile. "Could you just step over a couple of inches? That'd be great. Thanks!"

By nature, Ava was the cheery sort, but her perkiness seemed just a little too over the top. Wow, was she was nervous?

Because of him?

Right, like you're the center of the universe. Get real.

Caleb took a few steps forward until he was certain he was no longer blocking her shot of Santa Zach holding a regal-looking Pekingese. "How's this?"

"Super duper." She gave him a thumbs-up and dialed the wattage on her sunflower smile to stun. "Thanks a million."

Two little boys, chasing after a small dog,

smacked into his back and Caleb almost toppled over. Their mom corralled them, admonishing the boys to apologize, which they did, but he was rattled.

Find a safe place to land and stick. His mantra from every first day of the twelve different new schools he'd attended as a kid.

Better yet? Walk out. Ava was here, she could pick up the dogs for her parents.

Ah, but Ava was clearly working, and he'd promised Ted and Marjorie.

Right. Dang, his cowboy code of honor. When he made a promise, Caleb stuck to it no matter what. *Unlike some people.*

His gaze strayed back to Ava.

She was busy behind the camera, paying him no mind. He felt a tugging deep in his belly. Alarmed, he shook his head and turned away. Finally, he spied a small wooden chair tucked in the far corner next to the local librarian, Trudy Manfred.

Caleb strolled over and plunked down beside Trudy.

Two miniature pinschers wriggled in her arms. Trudy had dressed both dogs as reindeer, complete with brown felt antlers. In his opinion, they looked quite silly.

"Hi, Caleb," Trudy said. "Would you mind holding Buttons?"

The question appeared to be rhetorical since she'd already deposited Buttons in his lap. Still, manners required an answer. "Sure."

"It's nice Ava's back," Trudy said, happily patting her other dog. "Isn't it?"

Nice was the last word Caleb would have chosen. *Stressful* rose to mind. "Uh-huh."

Truth was, he breathed a lot easier when Ava stayed far away from Kringle. It might be her hometown and her parents lived here, but Ava Miller had caused him more worry than a coyote in a henhouse. She'd been his first girlfriend, his first love, and his first heartbreak.

But that was a decade ago.

Why was he reacting so strongly today? It wasn't as if he hadn't seen her at all over the last ten years. She returned to Kringle to visit her folks two or three times a year and since the Millers were his next-door neighbors, it was impossible to avoid her completely during those visits. But it wasn't as if he kept tabs on her or anything.

He could count on one hand the number of times they'd had an extended conversation since their broken engagement. If they saw each other around town, they were civil and made small talk. They were grown adults. No reason not to be civil.

Yet today, he was having an illogical physical reaction to her—galloping pulse, sweaty forehead, fluttery stomach.

Why?

He'd been caught off guard. That's all it was. Or who knew? Maybe he'd caught the flu.

The dog in his lap let out a small yip. Buttons was no happier about this hullabaloo than Caleb. He couldn't blame the little fella. The mini pinscher looked ridiculous in that reindeer outfit.

"Good boy." He scratched Buttons behind his ears and glanced over at Zach, who looked about as happy as a rancher could look when dressed as Santa.

Caleb would bet his favorite horse that some female had convinced poor Zach to put on that getup and his money was on Abby, the ten-year-old daughter of Zach's widowed friend, Suzannah Owens. Suzannah worked as a receptionist at the vet clinic.

Abby buzzed around the room like an industrious little bee, talking to people and petting animals. The kid was a social butterfly, just as Ava had been.

"You, me, and Zach are too agreeable," Caleb told Buttons.

The dog looked up at him with *don't-I-know-it* eyes.

"What was that?" Trudy peered at him over the rim of her glasses.

"It's your turn, Trudy," Ava announced. "Please arrange Buttons and Thimble in Santa's lap."

"Caleb?" Trudy asked. "Could you lend a hand?"

"Sure, sure." He helped Trudy get her dogs settled on poor Zach's lap for their picture and then scooted out of the frame.

He evaded Ava's gaze. He didn't need to see her. He knew what she looked like. Even after ten years, he still remembered every detail about her.

She was beautiful. Always had been and always would be in Caleb's eyes. She had a smile that lit up a room, soft honey-colored hair and amazing brown eyes that sparkled and danced with mirth ninety percent of the time. Ava liked to laugh, and she had a great one.

He missed her laugh most of all.

While Ava took the photos of Trudy's dogs on Santa's lap, Caleb sneaked a surreptitious peek her way. She was still the most stunning woman he'd ever seen. He had thought that from the moment he walked into freshman English at Kringle High School and headed for the back of the room.

On the way past her where she'd been sitting in the front row, his hip had brushed her elbow and he'd been a goner.

"Caleb, can you help Trudy to her car?" asked Dr. Chloe Anderson, the young vet who operated the Kringle Animal Clinic.

Caleb was a big fan of Chloe's. She was one smart cookie and she was terrific with his livestock—calm, sane, and sensible. He and Chloe had even dated briefly when she'd first moved to Kringle, but as much as they admired and respected each other, they both agreed they were too much alike to make a suitable match and they'd ended up just staying good friends.

"Sure thing," he said, taking Buttons from Zach as Trudy tucked tiny Thimble in the crook of her elbow and shouldered her oversized purse.

He and Buttons were becoming good pals. He looked down at the little dog. Buttons almost seemed to roll his eyes at the whole strange affair. Caleb chuckled at the Min Pin's expression.

"What's funny?" Ava asked brightly. "I want to laugh too."

"Nothing worth mentioning," he mumbled.

He kept his focus on Trudy and her dogs, helping the senior citizen get outside and settled in her car. As he turned to go back in, Trudy leaned out the open driver's side window and fixed him with a serious stare.

"You watch out, Caleb Sutton," Trudy said. "Lord knows, we all love Ava, but she's flighty as a hummingbird. Please take care of your heart and steer clear."

Huh? Had Trudy picked up on his uneasiness around Ava? Before he could ask her what she meant, the older woman gave him a quick pat on the cheek and put up her window.

Caleb watched her back out of the parking spot. Yeah, Trudy was right. No doubt about it. He agreed completely.

When it came to Ava Miller, he was treading lightly.

⸻

"Why don't we get some shots of the rescue dogs now?" Dr. Chloe said after the paying customers had dwindled.

The photography event had been about raising

extra money for the clinic to offer free spaying and neutering, where the locals could have pictures of their pets with Santa.

Chloe had contacted Ava months ago and recruited her as the photographer for when she came home for the holidays. Always up for a fun challenge, especially when the proceeds went to a noble cause, Ava had immediately said yes.

"Sure, sure." Ava blinked and turned from the window that looked out onto the parking lot where Caleb had gone with Trudy.

"Pining over Caleb?" Chloe teased with a twinkle in her eye. "He is one tall drink of water."

"No, no," she said, just a little too adamantly. "Just woolgathering."

"That's some mighty fine wool." Chloe chuckled.

"*Pfft.*" Ava waved a dismissive hand. "Caleb and I were over a decade ago."

"You sure?"

"Absolutely."

"You don't look so sure."

Really? What had Chloe picked up on? Could she tell Ava's heart rate kicked to the rafters when Caleb had bent over to put Buttons in his backseat harness, giving Ava a magnificent view of his backside? Chloe was a doctor after all, even if it was in veterinarian medicine.

"What's Caleb doing here?" Ava asked.

"Your parents brought in a couple of dogs for a comprehensive today," Chloe said. "Caleb is doing them a favor and picking them up while they're in Fort Worth at your dad's doctor's appointment."

"Oh," Ava said. She hadn't even known her dad had a doctor's appointment until she'd woken up that morning in her girlhood bed and found a note on the nightstand from her mother, telling Ava they'd gone to Fort Worth for a consultation with a specialist, but not to worry.

That made her worry even more.

She'd gotten into Kringle so late that her parents had been on their way to bed and they'd had little in the way of conversation. She couldn't help wondering why her folks hadn't asked her to pick up the animals on her way home from the photoshoot rather than roping Caleb into the task.

"Don't you normally go out to Kringle Kritters for intake examines on the strays?" Ava asked Chloe.

"Usually, yes, but I simply don't have a spare moment this week."

"Anything I can do to help?"

"Just take those brilliant pictures! I'll take Abby

and we'll bring in the rescue dogs for their time in front of the camera." Chloe winked and motioned for Abby to follow.

A few minutes later, Chloe and Abby brought in six dogs from the kennels. They were all on the scruffy side, as were most of the strays when they first arrived at Kringle Kritters Rescue.

"Let's give them a quick makeover," Ava said. "Glamour shots will increase their chances of getting adopted."

"Great idea!" Abby sang out and immediately started gathering scissors, combs, and brushes, along with handkerchiefs and bows to spruce them up.

"Hey, Caleb, wanna help?" Chloe called to Caleb, who'd ambled back inside.

Ava couldn't resist peeking over her shoulder. So far, Caleb had done a magnificent job of avoiding her. Did he feel as awkward around her as she felt around him?

Caleb looked uncomfortable. "Um, I've got—"

"Oh, please, please, please," Abby begged, pressing her palms together. "We need all the help we can get. These dogs are shaggy!"

No joke on that score.

"Twenty percent off your next vet bill," Chloe wheedled.

With a quick glance in Ava's direction, Caleb shrugged. "Sure, why not?"

"Yay, yay, yay!" Abby danced around the room.

Caleb met Ava's eyes directly for the first time. "This kid's unbridled enthusiasm reminds me a lot of you."

A compliment? From Caleb? Knock her over with a feather.

"Great!" Ava waved the FURminator grooming tool at him. "Why don't you brush the big guy. He's just your size. Make him handsome and debonair."

Caleb arched an eyebrow and looked down at the unkempt mixed breed whose mismatched appearance suggested a heritage from German shepherd, collie, pit bull, and Labrador stock and then back at Ava. "That's a tall order, peanut."

Peanut.

Her heart stuttered. *Wh-what?* Caleb hadn't called her peanut since she'd returned his engagement ring and told him that at eighteen, she was simply too young to get married. The term of endearment was the last thing she expected from him, and he seemed equally surprised by his slip of the tongue. A brow-cleaving frown quickly replaced his impish grin.

"Tall order is an understatement." Chloe chortled. "While Waldo here is a fine fella, he's known more for his personality than his dashing good looks."

"Luckily, hard-luck cases are my specialty." Caleb held out his hand. "Brush?"

Ava extended the grooming tool designed for massive hair removal. For a whisper of a second, their fingers touched.

And Ava's nerve endings lit up. Just like that Ava was back in high school, feeling giddy, giggly, and girlish. Back when the slightest touch from Caleb was enough to send tingles dancing throughout her entire body. She'd been hopelessly in love with him back then, and for a while at least, he'd been hopelessly in love with her too.

But she'd killed that love dead when she'd broken his heart.

If Caleb felt anything from the touch of their hands, he didn't show it. Instead, he dutifully set about brushing the dog. He'd always been methodical and trustworthy, the dependable sort that you could rely on to complete a task well and on time. His plodding ways had been one of their key problems as a couple. She was a "get 'er done" type who liked to keep things moving.

She looked at the Chihuahua in Abby's arms. This dog had short dark fur, so she didn't need much grooming, but she was quivering all over and looked positively terrified.

Ava took the little dog from Abby and cuddled it against her chest.

"You're going to be just fine," she promised. Glancing over at Chloe, Ava asked, "What's this one's name?"

"That's Juliet."

Ava kissed the top of the Chihuahua's head. "Juliet, someone great will adopt you. I just know it. Let's take a super glamorous picture of you with bows and a Christmas doggy sweater."

She dressed up Juliet, then took her over to where Santa and Mrs. Claus had just returned from a brief break. Zach and Suzannah were good sports to pose with the dogs, freely giving their time as she was.

"Santa, Juliet is very nervous and maybe a little cold," Ava said, taking off the red-and-white-striped candy cane hat she'd been wearing, and with Suzannah's help, posed Juliet in Zach's lap so it looked as if the dog was popping out of the hat like a perfect Christmas surprise.

"Hold that pose." Ava scurried to her camera and snapped a round of shots.

A peek through the viewing pane showed her

just how adorable Juliet looked. There was a splendid home in Juliet's future; Ava could feel it.

"Hey!" Abby said. "I just had a terrific idea. What if Kringle Kritters Rescue threw a big adoption party so that the pets could have new homes for the holiday?"

Dr. Chloe made a face. "I hate to toss water on your suggestion, sweet pea, but pushing pet adoption for Christmas can lead to impulsive adoption and that worries me. People who adopt need to prepare for a long commitment."

"We could set parameters in place to reduce spur-of-the-moment adoptions." Ava snapped her fingers. "I've got it. We could have a foster-to-adopt program so that people can be sure it's the right move for them before fully committing. Would that ease some of your concerns?"

Chloe nodded. "You might be onto something."

"Let's do it," Ava said, gung-ho to get started and find these sweet pets a forever home.

"Do you think your parents would be up for it on short notice?" Chloe asked.

That question gave her pause. While her mother's note said Dad's trip to the specialist was not a big deal, what if there was something wrong? Uneasy, she bit her bottom lip. "I'm home for the holidays. I could run the event with a little help from you guys."

"Ooh, ooh." Abby clapped her hands and jumped up and down. You could call it Home for the Holidays!"

"I like the way you think," Ava told the ten-year-old. "We could post the pictures we just took on the Kringle Kritters' website and write cute stories about each of the dogs. We could make individual posters for them all and put them in the stores and shops around town."

"That's a lot of work in a short amount of time," Caleb mumbled. "Are you sure you're up for it?"

Ava swung around to meet his intense gaze. He'd been so quiet that she'd almost forgotten he was there. "I am."

He snorted.

"What's that sound about?"

"Nothing."

"It's something or you wouldn't have done it. What's on your mind, Sutton?"

"It's just that you have a tendency to get caught in the moment's excitement, but when the going gets tough..." He trailed off and shook his head.

Ouch. That comment stung, but she understood how he might see things that way.

"I've got this." To prove it, Ava rolled up her sleeve and flexed her bicep like Wonder Woman. The event could be a tremendous hit, and with her parents' shelter almost at capacity, it would be nice to find homes for some of the rescues.

"I wanna help!" Abby said.

"Count me in." Chloe gave a thumbs-up.

Ava turned to look at the laconic cowboy brushing Waldo into a fine furry fellow. "Caleb? You in?"

He glanced up from where he'd crouched beside the stray. He had the most amazing eyes and Ava felt her heart flip into her throat.

Caleb's eyes were pale gray and paired with his coal-black hair, it was a devastating combo. He really was the poster boy for tall, dark, and handsome fantasy man. And even ten years later, she still wasn't immune.

She didn't know if she would ever be.

"Yeah, I'll help," he said, but his tone was flat. Perfunctory.

He was going to help because he was a good person. He would help because he felt it was the right thing to do, and Caleb Sutton always tried to do the right thing. Even if he didn't want to. Even if he'd rather do anything else. Caleb was that kind of guy. He'd help because he was dependable.

She could work with that.

"Cool," she said, taking Waldo's leash and walking him over to have his picture taken with Santa. On the way, she shot one last parting glance at Caleb.

He was frowning, which oddly made him look even more attractive, and picking up the balls of loose dog hair he'd brushed off Waldo.

Yep, she definitely could work with dependable. It might take some time—and some concerted effort —but she would get Caleb to forgive her.

After ten years of trotting the globe, she realized the most important thing in the world was goodwill and good people.

And despite their differences, Caleb was one of the best she'd ever met.

CHAPTER 2

WOULD THIS DAY *NEVER* END?

Once Caleb finished helping at the animal clinic, he drove the dogs back to Kringle Kritters Rescue. The only bright spot? He'd left Ava—and the complicated feelings she'd stirred in him—in his rearview mirror.

The dog kennels were in a small steel and concrete building just a few yards from the Millers' modest home. They built the house from light-red bricks and the roof was deep black. Out front was a large wooden sign with the shelter's name and their logo. Ava had designed that logo back in high school. He'd been there the day she'd come up with it.

The sign, he noted, could use a fresh coat of paint.

The temperature was in the low fifties, so it was cool enough and far more manageable to unload his truck one dog at a time.

He opened the smallest portable kennel nestled in the extended cab, picked up little Juliet, and carried her into the shelter.

The sounds of crazed barking greeted him along with the sight of a real Christmas tree decorated with pet-themed items—doggie treats, bells, bows, chew toys—that put the scent of pine in the air.

"Hey, there." Ted, in red-and-green suspenders, faded blue jeans, a plaid, long-sleeved shirt, and a Panama hat strolled over. Ted was a thin man with a full head of bushy white hair and eyebrows to match.

"How'd it go at the doctor?" Caleb asked.

"Fine, fine. Just getting older." Ted popped his suspenders and grinned. "It's no big deal beyond having to drive to Fort Worth to see the specialist."

Caleb didn't want to pry into Ted's personal business, so he changed the subject. "Hey, I've got a bone to pick with the two of you."

"What's up?" Ted asked.

Trying not to frown and give away just how much Ted's daughter had affected him, Caleb cleared his throat. "Why didn't you tell me Ava was taking pictures at the clinic today?"

Ted didn't meet Caleb's gaze. "Is that a fact?"

"You know it is." It annoyed Caleb that the Millers were playing games with him. "You should have told me. I had no idea she was home for the holidays already. Usually she doesn't arrive until the week of Christmas."

Ted shrugged casually. "She's a grown woman. We don't keep tabs on her."

"All you had to do was say, hey, Caleb, Ava's in town for Christmas and she's taking pet pictures at the clinic. I could have prepared myself."

"You're right, we should have told you," said Marjorie.

"Yes." Caleb was determined not to sound petulant, but someone who was merely setting good boundaries. "You should've."

"I know seeing Ava is hard on you." Marjorie clucked her tongue.

He waved a hand, appreciating the Millers' concern. But it had been ten years, and he wasn't still carrying a torch for their only child. "Water, bridge, I'm over it. What happened between Ava and me is ancient history."

"Whew!" Ted ran the back of his hand over his forehead as if wiping off sweat. "You have no idea how good it feels to hear you say that."

"You mean a lot to us, Caleb. Never forget that."
Marjorie got up and came around the desk to join
them.

Like her husband, Marjorie was in her early
sixties and also had a head full of flowing white hair
that she pulled back from her forehead with a whim-
sical butterfly barrette more suited for a schoolgirl
than someone her age, but gave her a carefree,
youthful air. It was clear where Ava had gotten her
quirky sense of style.

"How'd this little gal do?" Marjorie asked, taking
Juliet from Caleb. "We just took her in yesterday
morning."

"She trembled a lot, but Abby Owens was there,
and they hit it off big-time," Caleb said.

"Juliet's a little skittish." Marjorie made kissing
noises at the Chihuahua, who wagged her tail wildly,
lapping up the love.

"I'll bring in the rest of the dogs," Caleb said,

He couldn't stay irritated with the Millers. They
were agreeable people who did a terrific job helping
homeless animals. They also were his friends and
they loved their daughter, even though they didn't
agree with some of the things she did.

Like dumping Caleb right before the wedding.

Gritting his teeth at the memory, he gathered the

leashes of the other dogs, clipped them to their collars and after some finagling, managed to get the animals inside the shelter. One by one, Ted and Marjorie took the dogs from him and lead them to the kennels. Each time the door opened, more crazed barking ensued.

Once they'd penned the dogs, Marjorie and Ted returned to the intake area.

"No help today?" Caleb asked, more from common courtesy than any genuine desire to know their staffing issues.

"Len's dad broke his leg and he went home to San Antonio to see him," Marjorie said, referring to the young man who usually walked the dogs daily and did the grooming. "And Charlotte had already asked for the holidays off because she and her husband are taking a belated honeymoon."

Charlotte was in her mid-fifties and married to a local farmer. She answered the phone and kept the books. And she'd been with the Millers from the inception of Kringle Kritters Rescue thirty years earlier.

"Huh?" Caleb stared at her. "Like a second honeymoon? Charlotte and Jim got married when dirt was invented."

Ted chuckled. "Marj and I thought the same

thing, but Charlotte said they never had a real honeymoon, so now that their kids are grown and gone, they went on a cruise and called it their honeymoon. They even booked the honeymoon suite with a big fancy balcony and everything."

"We never had a real honeymoon," Marjorie murmured. "Maybe one day we could take a cruise."

It seemed a little strange to Caleb to go on a honeymoon thirty years after the wedding, but hey, what did he know about long-lasting marriages?

"I guess better late than never," he said, aware that both Ted and Marjorie were watching him. Tension lay in the room, as thick as the barking from the kennels. Anytime weddings, marriage, or honeymoons came up whenever he was around the Millers, things got stiff.

Might as well deal with it. Taking the bull by the horns, Caleb inhaled deeply and tackled the dreaded subject.

"Sooo..." He exhaled a hiss of air. "Ava's back."

Ted nodded, slow and deliberate, as if the motion took a great deal of concentration. "Yep. She's in between jobs."

Marjorie placed one hand on Caleb's arm and looked up into his face with a pitying expression. "To tell you the truth, she surprised us. We had no idea she was coming home this early. She just walked in the front door last night after texting us from the airport that she was on the way. I supposed we were so stunned to see her, and what with Ted's doctor's appointment in Fort Worth this morning, we didn't think about telling you."

Caleb wasn't buying it, but he let Marjorie have her excuse and didn't press.

"Not that we aren't thrilled she's come home," Ted added quickly. "It's great to have Ava back in the nest anytime."

"She's staying with you?" Usually, when Ava came back to town, she booked a room at the Kringle Inn because her parents' house was small and she didn't want to inconvenience them.

Ted and Marjorie exchanged uneasy glances, and Caleb knew something was up. He braced himself, curling his fingers into fists. "What?"

"It's just that, um..." Ted trailed off, lifting his hat to scratch his head and looking over at his wife.

That left Caleb wondering if the older man's mind was slipping or if he simply didn't know how to break bad news.

"Um." Ted lifted his hat again to thread his hand through his thick thatch of hair.

"Yes?" Caleb's entire body tightened with tension.

"Do we tell him now?" Marjorie asked her husband. "Or should we wait until after the holidays?"

"No," Caleb said. "You don't get to do that. You can't infer there's bad news and then clam up about it."

"He's right," Ted told his wife. "He deserves to know."

"Are you sure you don't want an ignorance-is-bliss Christmas?" From the look on Marjorie's face, Caleb had a feeling he was absolutely not going to like what she said next.

"Please, just tell me."

Ted blew out his breath. "We'll tell you, but you have to promise not to tell Ava. We want her to have one last holiday in the house she grew up in."

This did not sound good. Did he really want to know? If it was bad news, how could he not tell Ava?

Cowboy up, Sutton. They looked as if they desperately needed to share their news with someone.

"I won't tell Ava anything you share with me in confidence," he promised.

Ted and Marjorie looked at each other.

"Do you want to tell him?" Ted asked his wife.

"It's your news to tell."

Even before the words were out of Ted's mouth, Caleb knew what he would say.

Ted took a deep breath, held it for several seconds, and then said on a long exhale, "I have melanoma skin cancer." He rushed to add, "But it's okay. They caught it early. I don't even have to have chemo. They'll just remove it and the cure rate at this stage is almost one hundred percent."

Caleb placed a hand to his chest. "Thank the Lord."

"Ted is going to be fine," Marjorie said. "But this scare has changed the way we look at things."

"While we love running the rescue..." Ted hooked both thumbs around his suspenders. "We realized we haven't really had much of a life outside of taking care of animals and raising Ava. Since she's grown and gone and shows no signs of settling down and giving us grandkids or taking over the shelter, we've decided it's time for us to live a little."

"You've been thinking about this for a while," Caleb said.

"About a year," Marjorie nodded. "Ted's diagnosis just cinched the deal."

"We're going to close the shelter and sell the house," Ted said.

"And we've already rented a house in town. It has a big backyard and it's close to the grocery store." Marjorie took hold of her husband's hand.

"Wow," Caleb said. "This is all happening so fast. I don't know what to say."

"Be happy for us." Marjorie's smile was bittersweet. "While letting go of the place is a big deal, we're very excited about the future."

"And damn happy I got such a gentle wake-up call," Ted added. "It could have been so much worse."

Before Caleb could find the appropriate response to this life-altering news, a fresh cacophony of barking erupted from the kennels.

"I wonder what that's about," Ted mumbled, heading for the door with Marjorie and Caleb at his heels.

Before Ted could open it, Ava walked into the room.

"Yikes, they sure are noisy." Ava grinned, shrugged, and did a comical dancing two-step that had once endeared her to Caleb. She was still wearing the silly candy cane costume and carrying her camera equipment. "I shouldn't have come in through the back door. You'd think I was a burglar or something. I guess they don't remember me."

How can they remember you? You show up here three times a year at most.

"Oh!" Ava's eyes widened as she took him in. "It's you."

"Yeah, it's me." His tone came out flinty and clipped. Not what he intended.

Ava looked as if she wanted to back up, fly through the kennels, and stir up the dogs again in hopes the barking would drown out everything.

"I've got to prep Bullet's food." Marjorie took a step toward the front door. "That old bulldog has severe allergies and dental issues. Chloe gave me a special formula to cook for him."

"I'll help," Ted said, gingerly following in his wife's footsteps.

They shut the door behind them, leaving Caleb alone with Ava. He didn't know why he didn't just leave. Nothing was holding him here beyond Ava's beseeching eyes.

What would be her response when she discovered her father had cancer and her parents were closing the shelter and selling her girlhood home? Would she, too, have an epiphany and want to come home to be near her parents? Or would she continue in her wanderlust ways?

Bigger question, why did he care?

Honestly, it was none of his concern. While the Millers were fantastic neighbors and he had great affection for them, his world wouldn't change much. New neighbors would move in, and life would go on.

And yet, Ted's news rattled him. He viewed the Millers as a permanent fixture in his life and he'd almost become their son-in-law. He'd known them for fourteen years and assumed he'd know them for many more.

Now, everything was up in the air.

"How you doing, peanut?" he asked, his heartstrings tugging for Ava.

She gave him a weird look. "I should ask you that question. You look as if you've just come from a funeral."

"No problems in my sphere."

Narrowing her eyes, she regarded him with suspicion. "I'm fine. Why wouldn't I be?"

He cast around for a decent reason to cloak his feelings. He'd promised Ted and Marjorie he wouldn't tell Ava what was going on, but if he didn't get control over his emotions, she'd ferret out that something was afoot. Despite her flighty nature, Ava was pretty perceptive, and Caleb was a rotten liar.

"You sure volunteered to put together a massive adoption event on short notice," he said. "I don't know how you're going to pull it off."

"What do you mean? I've been working at this shelter my entire life. Fundraising is in my DNA. I—"

"That's not true. You've been gone for ten years."

"But I come home—"

"Two or three times a year."

"Usually for several weeks at a time and I always work at the shelter when I visit."

Caleb snorted.

"What is it, Mr. Snorty Snort-Snort?"

"You have no idea what's going on around here," he said. The minute the words were out of his mouth, he realized he'd said too much.

"Wait, what?" She came closer, her smile completely gone now. "Is there something you're not telling me?"

"You're taking on too much. You're only home for a few weeks. You should spend time with your parents instead of throwing an impromptu event that would normally take months to plan—"

Ava rolled her eyes hard. "You haven't changed

one little whit, Caleb. Always planning, preparing, getting ready. When will your life ever start?"

That was a dagger right through his heart. His hurt must have shown on his face.

She slapped a palm over her mouth. "I'm sorry. I shouldn't have said that."

"You're entitled to your feelings."

"I was irritated. You are who you are. It's not my place to judge you and it's really not your place to judge me either."

"You're right. We're so different. It's hard for us to see the other person's perspective."

"We're night and day."

"You gallivant." He offered a small smile to lighten things up.

"You root." She anted up a brighter smile than his.

"You're a butterfly."

"You're a tree."

"Good thing we didn't get married," he mumbled.

"Good thing," she echoed.

"Look," he said. "Something we can finally agree on."

"Yay us."

Her gaze hit his with the impact of a sledgehammer. "I better get to work."

"Me too."

"Bye," she said without moving.

"So long." He didn't move either, and instead watched the pulse at her neck tick.

"See you around."

He had to get out of here before he told her about her father. "Take care, Ava."

Her expression shifted from one of pugnacious levity to suspicion. "You're not acting right, Sutton. What's up?"

"Nothing. I'm just afraid your Home for the Holidays event will be a big bust."

"So what if it is? At least I'll take a shot."

He notched up his chin and narrowed his eyes. "Meaning?"

"Sometimes, Cabe, you've simply got to act." And with that, she turned on her heel and walked back into the kennels, setting off a fresh cacophony of barking.

CHAPTER 3

CALEB'S COMMENTS got under Ava's skin. She tried not to think about him as her mother showed her around the kennels the following day, introducing her to the dogs she'd be trying to find homes for during the impromptu holiday event she and Abby Owens had created on the spot.

While following her spontaneous impulses occasionally landed her in trouble, more often than not, there was a serendipitous quality to action. Taking calculated risks usually set her on the path to adventure that almost always worked out in her favor.

The journey might not be smooth, but hey, the bumps in the road were where the interesting things lurked, right?

Caleb had never understood that. He believed

you shouldn't roll over in bed without a plan and that attitude, in her estimation, killed the thrill of discovery.

"You've added more kennels since last year," Ava observed as they strolled the facility.

"Yes, we can house sixty dogs in here. The cat kennels next door can take double that. We took out the closet and converted the space into two dozen extra kennels and had the shed out back installed for storage. The shelter has grown a lot since you...um... took a detour with your life."

Ava sighed. Her mother was tiptoeing around ancient history. Why? The past was over and done with.

"Mom, I left," Ava said. "Just accept it. I was supposed to marry Caleb, and instead, I walked away to travel the world. I was eighteen years old. I wasn't ready to get married. I loved Caleb with all my heart, but I didn't know who I was."

"Do you know now?" her mother asked softly.

"Yes, I do."

"And what is that?"

"I understand how I fit into the world. From behind a camera, photographing the far corners of the world, I've gained perspective on my life that I would never have gotten if I'd stayed in Kringle."

"Can you sum it up for me?"

Ava tapped her chin. "I discovered people are the same no matter where you go. They all want the same things. To be happy and safe and loved."

"Caleb loved you."

"I know, but I until I left town, I couldn't trust my feelings. I'd only loved one man. I had nothing to compare it to."

"And now you do?"

Ava had spent the last ten years on the road. She'd had a handful of romances. She'd had fun. She'd enjoyed herself, but she had found no one who meant as much to her as Caleb once had. Sometimes that kept her awake at night, thinking about what she'd thrown away. Ironic that the only way to know what she'd had was to walk away from it.

"I appreciate that you've grown so much as a person, done so much with your life already, but honey, I'm so worried about your future. Are you going to spend the rest of your life roaming the world alone?"

Ava had no idea.

"Don't worry." Ava hugged her mom. "I'm okay. I promise. I was young. I was impulsive. I wasn't ready to settle down in Kringle. I wanted to see the world and I did. Mission accomplished."

"Does that mean you're finally ready to settle down?" her mother asked hopefully.

Ava shrugged. Truthfully, she was at a crossroads in her life. She'd lost her last job due to the company she worked for going out of business and nothing new had shown up, although she'd applied to three jobs in three different countries and was waiting to hear back.

"I'm taking some time off from work."

"Oh, my!" her mother exclaimed, looking so happy that Ava felt a bit guilty. She knew leaving Kringle had hurt her and Dad as much as it had hurt Caleb. "That's fabulous. How long will you be staying?"

"I'm not sure. Definitely through the new year."

"I see." Her mother looked disappointed. "I thought maybe you meant you were going to take six months or a year away from the travel."

"I'm playing it by ear, if that's okay. Don't worry, I won't be in your hair. I'll rent a place in town."

"You'll do no such thing. This is your home. You'll stay right here."

"And help with the shelter."

"We'd love that so much."

"Me too, Mom. Me too."

"I'm so glad you're home." Her mother held out her arms.

Ava hugged her mother amidst the serenade of barking dogs.

"While we're in a hugging mood, do you want to hug the animals? It's time for their daily cuddles."

"Absolutely. I thought you'd never ask." Ava giggled.

"Let's start with Moses and Tiny." Her mother crouched in front of the kennel containing an elderly basset hound and nodded for Ava to free the Great Dane from the oversized pen behind her.

"C'mon, Tiny," Ava said, suspecting that her father had named the dog.

Sometimes the rescues came in as nameless strays, and Ted Miller was famous for giving them ironic monikers. Other times, as with Moses, the pets were owner surrendered. Her mother had already told her that Moses' owner, a local elderly woman who used to teach art at Kringle High, had developed Alzheimer's and could no longer care for him.

Only three kennels remained unoccupied out of the sixty available. Ava petted the lively Tiny, who wagged his massive tail so hard it slammed into Ava's mother's back.

"Whoa," her mother said, laughing. "Turn Tiny

out into the dog run, would you, sweetheart? He's only two years old and has boundless energy."

"Will do." Ava reached for one of the many cheap, multi-colored leashes her parents hung on wall pegs around the kennels. The place was as full as Ava had ever seen it, and she hoped the Home for the Holidays event would help place many of the animals in loving homes.

She led Tiny to the dog run and released him into the enclosure, where he immediately started running around and around the pen as fast as his long legs would carry him.

Wow, she thought. *He looks a lot like me when I first left Kringle, crazed with pent-up energy and so certain I was going somewhere when I just ran in circles.*

Mom brought out Moses, and they let the two dogs romp for a while before returning them to their kennels. Next, they visited Juliet.

The little dog was curled in a ball on a blanket in the corner of her kennel, but when she saw Ava, her face lit up. She ran to the cage door, wriggling so vigorously it looked as if she'd topple right over.

"You have an admirer," her mother murmured.

Ava opened the kennel and picked up Juliet. She

had to admit, the little dog had wiggled her way into her heart.

"I think she and I have a special bond." She looked at her mom.

"Too bad your nomadic lifestyle prevents you from adopting her."

"No, but if *you* adopted her, I could see her every time I came home."

"Sweetheart, do I need to remind you we've already adopted five dogs?"

"No." Ava chuckled. "They all came in bouncing on my bed this morning."

"My fault. I shouldn't allow them on the furniture, but I can't resist." Laughing, her mother brushed dog hair off her sleeve. "I have too much love to give and it's hard for me to get down on the floor and romp with them the way I used to romp with you."

It had been fun growing up at the shelter. Because she'd always had so many animals around, she'd never felt the lack of siblings. She'd had an idyllic childhood, and her travels had only underscored how lucky she'd been to have such loving parents who'd always put her needs ahead of their own.

Ava gave Juliet a kiss on the top of her head. "I'll be back soon."

Juliet looked at Ava with solemn eyes and blinked twice, almost as if she understood the plan.

After they finished spending time with every animal, Ava and her mother headed to the office where her father was working on the computer.

He looked up and smiled as they entered the room. "So what's the verdict? Do you think we can pull off this Home for the Holidays thing by next Friday?"

"Sure!" Ava said. "What's the worst that can happen? No one shows up and we're no worse off than we were before, minus the money I spent on advertising."

Her parents looked at each other in that way that long-married couples did but they didn't say a word.

"Here are the posters you asked me to print up." Her father took a stack of papers off the full color printer and handed them to Ava.

She studied the poster she'd stayed up late to create.

They looked good if she did say so herself. She'd used Juliet's picture popping from the Christmas stocking for the advertising. No way around it— Juliet looked cute as the dickens. Later, she would photograph all the pets at the shelter and make a similar poster for each one of them.

"She's so darling," her mother said. "Juliet looks amazing in this photograph! You've done a superb job with this, Ava."

Ava had written a brief story to go along with the picture, explaining that Juliet was a cheerful, friendly dog who loved to help—hence her job as Santa's elf. Juliet would fit in well in any home because she got along with children and pets alike.

The bottom part of the poster explained the goal of Home for the Holidays. They scheduled the big adoption event the day after the town's parade, so that meant there would be plenty of people in town for the Christmas tree lighting festival. They encouraged folks to come sooner and qualify to adopt a new family member. Ava hoped the big push would help empty the shelter before Christmas. What a lofty goal.

"Let me see if I can place these posters around town."

"Want me to help?" her mother asked.

Ava started to say yes, but she knew her mother well enough to spot a shift in tone. Her mother was sincerely offering to help, but she really didn't want to.

"I've got this."

"If you're sure..." Her mother and father exchanged another cryptic look, and she couldn't help wondering what they were thinking. Worried about their flighty daughter no doubt.

For the first time since she'd left home, Ava wondered if maybe their concerns about her future were valid.

———

The UPS truck disappeared out of sight just as Caleb realized one of the packages the driver had delivered was dog food destined for Kringle Kritters. It had gotten mixed in with his order of horse and cattle feed.

He could have one of his hands drive it over, but they were out mending fences and would be at it all day. No bother to hop into his truck and take it over to the Millers'. He wasn't doing it in the hope of seeing Ava again. He was simply being neighborly.

Your nose will grow, Sutton, if you keep that up.

Not true. He would take the feed over whether Ava was there or not.

Yes, but you wouldn't jump to it immediately.

Fine. Seeing Ava again had stirred old feelings,

both good and bad. He'd spent a restless night thinking about her and wishing for things better not wished for. She was who she was. A free bird. And darn if he didn't love that about her.

She was fearless. And even though her bravery scared him, he respected it. Respected her. How many other eighteen-year-old girls raised in a small rural town took off for adventure with only a talent for photography and an optimistic attitude that everything would work out as it should?

So many things could have gone wrong. He'd even made a list and given it to her before she took off. But she was fairy dusted and everything had worked out in her favor. Secretly, a part of himself that he wasn't particularly proud of, had hoped she'd fall on her face and come running back home with her tail between her legs.

It had taken him a good year to shake off that wishful thinking and accept that she wasn't coming back.

When he pulled up in front of the shelter, all three Millers were running around behind their main house. The gate to their backyard stood open.

A feeling of dread settled over Caleb. He knew trouble when he saw it. Once or twice in the past, the Millers' pets had gotten out of the gate, usually because one of the volunteers had forgotten to shut the gate between the house and the shelter. If the dogs had taken off, they could end up anywhere on his ranch and he owned a couple of donkeys who were used to battling coyotes and were aggressive to canines.

Or worse, they could end up on the road.

Caleb parked and jumped from his truck. "What's up?"

Ted rushed over to him. "I'd let the dogs out in the backyard when I came over to the shelter, and I guess my mind, my mind. I forgot to lock the gate behind me. I'm a feeble old sot."

Caleb didn't comment. He knew what it looked like when a guy was raking himself over the coals. Ted Miller wasn't the least bit feeble, and Caleb suspected Ted's lapse had nothing to do with memory loss and everything to do with his recent cancer diagnosis. Even if it was a very curable cancer, your own mortality was a scary thing to face.

"These things happen," Caleb soothed. "It'll be all right. How many dogs got out?"

Rubbing a hand over his thinning pate, Ted's voice filled with panic. "All five of them."

Face flushed, the older man leaned over and

braced his palms against his knees to catch his breath.

"Dad?" Ava rushed over. "Are you okay?"

"Fine." Ted panted and waved away his daughter's concern. "Just got a little winded."

Caleb shifted his gaze to Marjorie. She was almost as breathless as her husband and despite the cold air, perspiration dewed her brow.

"Let me." Caleb reached for the five leashes Ted clutched in one hand.

Ted relinquished them without argument.

Caleb raised his head and his gaze landed on Ava.

She nodded.

He didn't bother to run his idea by her. The look she'd given him told Caleb they agreed. "Ava and I will round up the dogs. This shouldn't take us long."

"C'mon, you old coot," Marjorie teased and took her husband's hand. "Let the young'uns do their thing."

"I'm not that old," Ted grumbled, but he followed his wife into the shelter's office.

"I'm guessing that none of your parents' pets respond to a whistle?" Caleb asked Ava.

"Probably not." Ava offered a wry smile. "They

raised their dogs the way they raise their daughter, with a gentle hand."

"That's nice," he said. "The world could use more gentle hands."

"I probably could have used more discipline and structure," she mused, holding his gaze for a second too long.

Was there some significance in her statement? Was she confessing something to him? Was there an apology in there somewhere? Caleb held his breath, but she didn't continue that thread of conversation.

Instead, Ava stuck the fingers of both hands into her mouth and let loose with a long, loud, ear-splitting whistle.

Caleb jumped. "Where did you learn to do that?"

Ava grinned. "A chocolatier in the Swiss Alps. I was photographing h—"

He held up a palm. "Wait, wait. I don't need to hear about your sexual adventures with another man."

"*Her...*" Ava said pointedly.

"You had sexual adventures with a woman?" he asked, surprised but intrigued.

"Don't be such a guy. My sexual adventures have all been pretty tame. Anyway, the chocolatier's name is Astrid Aubry and I was filming her for a Sprüngli shoot."

"I have no idea what that is."

"Sprüngli is a famous Swiss chocolatier and they needed new content for their updated website."

"That's the kind of photography you were doing? For websites."

"Sure." She canted her head and studied him. "What did you think I was doing?"

"I dunno." Caleb felt sheepish. "Photojournalism, I guess."

"That's what I'd intended when I left Kringle," Ava said. "But my career took a different path and I'm a much better photographer than I am a writer."

"You could have stayed local if all you wanted to do was generate content for websites. I thought..." He trailed off. "I'm sorry that sounded passive aggressive."

Instead of responding, Ava whistled for the dogs again.

Feeling shamefaced, Caleb decided that apologizing had made a bigger deal of his pettiness than it deserved. "Hang on, I'll go home and get my ATV."

"Give them time to respond to my whistles."

He moved closer to her, still clutching the leashes. "Who do you think will appear first?"

"Most likely Stephen King," she said. "He can't stay away from Mom too long."

Another whistle from Ava and finally a black Labrador retriever came charging through the coastal fields on Caleb's property. He shimmied right under the fence and wandered over, looking relaxed and happy.

"Hey, boy." Caleb crouched and gently patted the ground in front of him at the same time he opened the clasp on one leash.

"Hey there, Stephen King," Ava murmured.

"Named after your dad's favorite author?"

Ava grinned. "You've got it."

Stealthily, in case Stephen King bolted, Caleb slipped the leash clap around the ring on the dog's collar.

"One down," he said to Ava. "Four to go."

She flashed him a genuine smile. "You haven't lost your touch with animals, that's for sure. I never met a dog who didn't adore you."

He shrugged. It hadn't been a big deal.

"What should we do now?" she asked.

"Go over to my place and get the ATV we use for herding cattle. We can cover more ground." He didn't mention the donkeys. He didn't want to freak her out.

"Thank you."

He'd been heading toward his truck, but at her gratitude, he turned and glanced at her. The same old pull he always felt whenever he looked at Ava tugged at his solar plexus. It bothered him that he was still so attracted to her. Man, he had the common sense of a rock.

"It's not a problem," he said and passed the Lab's leash to her. "Why don't you take Stephen King inside, and then we'll hit my place for the ATV and make quick work of this."

Ava nodded, and then out of the blue she said, "You know I'm sorry, right? I never meant to hurt you."

Now wasn't the time to discuss *that* topic. Heck, he wasn't sure he ever wanted to discuss the past with her.

"Let's focus on the dogs," he said. Because of the mixed-up feelings churning inside him, it was all he could manage.

CHAPTER 4

AFTER DROPPING Stephen King off with her parents in the shelter, Ava jumped into Caleb's truck and they took off down the rural road back to his place.

The minute she settled into the seat she was acutely aware of him and the tension stretching between them thick as pulled taffy.

For a farm truck, the vehicle was surprisingly clean, but then again, Caleb had always been tidy. There was a bit of dirt on the floorboard, the smell of livestock feed in the air, and a thin layer of dust on the dashboard, but it wasn't junky with supplies or empty containers or product wrappers like her dad's work pickup. She noticed the interior because it was easier than noticing the man.

Hesitantly, she lifted her gaze to study Caleb's handsome profile—masculine nose, firm chin, sharp cheekbones. He wore a black felt cowboy hat pulled low on his forehead, and it hid the lush fall of dark hair she knew was beneath it. He wore faded Wranglers, plain brown Justin boots, and a red flannel work shirt underneath a shearling jacket.

He looked like what he was. A dyed-in-the-wool cowboy.

Some things never changed. But here was the deal. Where she'd once found her small country town and the folks in it dull and staid, after traveling the world she had a whole new perspective and a deep respect for the things and people she'd left behind.

At eighteen, she'd been cavalier, not appreciating what she'd had and believing the wide world at large had more to offer her than the community where she'd grown up. Instead of treasuring who she was and where she came from, she'd dismissed it as colloquial and pedestrian. What she'd learned was that people were the same all over the world, and just because something was different and seemed exotic to her, it didn't make it better than Kringle.

Living with this lesson was ironic when she was sitting in the man's truck. The man she'd left behind.

The man who could still turn her world upside down with a lazy grin.

Heavens, she'd been such a foolish young girl when she'd broken his heart. Guilt nibbled at her. How could she have treated his love so casually? Had she secretly believed that he'd just been waiting around for her to return for good?

If so, that was pretty damn selfish. Ava cringed.

Quickly, she dispelled any notion that she had a future with Caleb. It was too late for them.

Losing him was the price she'd paid to find herself. She'd needed time to determine what she wanted in life. Caleb might have known from an early age that he wanted to stay on his grandfather's ranch and raise horses and longhorns, but Ava hadn't a clue what she'd wanted from life...

Or love.

Now she knew, but it was too late.

Stop beating yourself up, Ava.

If she hadn't left Kringle, she never would have discovered who she was as a photographer, and she wouldn't have built a successful career. She'd needed time, and even though she knew she'd hurt Caleb badly, it had been the right thing for them both.

They crested a small hill, and in the distance,

Ava spied a small brown dog wandering aimlessly in a field near the road.

"Look, there's Minnie Pearl." She pointed.

Slowing, Caleb guided the truck into the bar ditch near the fence and parked. Ava tumbled out, leash in hand.

Minnie Pearl saw her and came running, eager for rescue.

"Did those longer-legged dogs run off and leave you behind, babe?" Ava cooed, squatting beside the dachshund and clicking the leash clasp around her collar.

Scooping Minnie Pearl into her arms, she opened the rear door and deposited the dog inside and secured her with the doggy seat belt that Caleb used for transporting his ranch dogs. She had to adjust the straps for Minnie's small size.

"Two down, three to go," she declared, returning to the passenger seat. "I wonder where the others went."

Caleb took off his Stetson and ran a hand through his hair.

Her pulse quickened at the sight of his wavy locks. Whether or not she admitted it, he still took her breath away.

"They might have wandered up to my house. My

housekeeper Freda is notorious for feeding strays." Caleb put the truck in gear, and they continued to his home.

Ava glanced over the seat to check on Minnie Pearl, who seemed content.

The old farmhouse that had belonged to Caleb's grandparents came into view and her breath caught at the sight of it. She had so many fond memories of the place—spring planting and summer harvest. Watermelons and fireworks on the Fourth of July. Picnics by the pond. Halloween parties and hayrides.

And of course Christmas.

It had been her favorite season on the Leaping Longhorn Ranch. His grandparents and mother had gone all out. Decorating as passionately as anyone in Kringle, and that was saying a lot for a town besotted with Christmas. In fact, the ranch had won the town decorating contest more than once. More memories tumbled in on her. She and Caleb helping string lights from the eaves, hanging stockings on the mantel, and kissing under the mistletoe.

Her cheeks heated and she turned her head so he wouldn't notice and studied the house. "You haven't decorated for Christmas! Why not? It's only two weeks away."

He shrugged. "No reason to decorate. Mom was

the Christmas fanatic. Without her, it's too much of an effort."

"You liked to decorate when we were teenagers."

"We're not kids anymore, Ava. Christmas is for children."

"And the young at heart," she said.

"That's you, not me," he grumbled.

"Ah, c'mon. Don't be a grinch. You should at least put up a few lights. It'll help you get into the holiday spirit."

"Nah. It's not really my thing anymore."

That made her feel so sad, as if he'd given up on the joys of life. Because of her? "Not even a tree inside?"

"Why put up decorations for a couple of weeks just to turn around and take them down again? Seems like a lot of unnecessary work."

Ava's mouth dropped open. "Caleb Sutton, I cannot believe you just said that. Why take a shower every day when you have to turn around and take another shower the next day? Why wash your truck when you know your truck is just going to get dirty again the next time you drive across a muddy field?"

He laughed and held up a hand. "Fine. Point made. I'll decorate. But only if you agree to pitch in."

She rewarded him with a grin. "Great. I'll get

some of my friends, and we'll come over tomorrow to help. Decorating is always more fun when you have a crowd. I'll even bring snacks. We'll make it a party. We—"

"Look there." Caleb gestured as he stopped the truck near the horse barn.

Two dogs—a German shepherd mix and an Aussiepoo were standing on their back legs drinking from the water trough.

"They look like drinking buddies bellied up to a bar." Ava laughed. "Felix and Oscar, the odd couple."

"You know all their names?"

"I do. They're my parents' pets. Mom talks about them endlessly."

He made a noise that was just short of a snort. "I didn't think you kept up with something that trivial."

"What must you think of me, Caleb? I'm interested in my parents' lives. I communicate with them regularly. We text every day, several times a day even."

"Why are you getting defensive?"

"I'm not." Was she? She lowered her voice and spoke more slowly to disprove his claim. "Do you think the dogs will come to me like Minnie Pearl did? These two don't know me very well and since they started off life as strays, they might still have a bit of wild to them."

"Let's stroll along as if catching them is the last thing we have in mind," Caleb suggested.

Ava chuckled. "Sneaky. I like it."

He laughed. "Stick with me. I have more tricks up my sleeve."

She'd missed that laugh so much. More than she realized. Maybe they *could* be friends after all. That would be so nice. They ambled closer toward the water trough, purposefully ignoring the dogs.

Ava cast around for a safe conversational topic. "How's your mom doing?"

Caleb's dad had died in a military operation when Caleb was fourteen. He and his mother Bethany had moved to Kringle to live with his mother's parents. His mom had stayed on the ranch after her parents passed away until a few years ago when she'd sold it to him, remarried, and moved to Dallas.

"Mom and Chet are so in love, it's fun to watch them together. They're like lovesick teenagers. He's a private pilot and they're always flying off to somewhere exciting. She got the travel bug the same way you did. After spending much of her life on a ranch, she's loving seeing the world, although most of the trips they take are in the US."

Ava kept one eye on the dogs, who were watching them with open curiosity. "Does your mom miss Kringle?"

Caleb stopped walking and crouched on the same level as the dogs, making himself less threatening. Following his lead, she hunkered beside him.

"She does," he said. "But she loves her more footloose life and says the only thing that will settle her down again is having grandchildren to fuss over."

The two dogs came closer, wagging their tails. Soon enough, their curiosity got the better of them and they inched closer to Caleb and Ava. Quick as a wink, they snapped the leashes to the dogs' collars.

Four down, one to go.

But Caleb's comment about his mother wanting grandchildren shook Ava. If she and Caleb had gotten married right out of high school, most likely they would be parents by now. Unexpected feelings stirred inside her—loss, remorse, and a bone-deep yearning.

Oh, she didn't regret spreading her wings and leaving Kringle to explore the world. What she did regret was hurting Caleb in the process. But she was no longer the headstrong teen she'd once been, and she needed him to forgive her.

Because what she wanted more than anything in

the world was a solid friendship with the man she'd left behind.

———

"Let's go get that last dog," Caleb said once they had Felix and Oscar in the truck alongside Minnie Pearl. The nippy December weather was cold enough so the animals would be okay in the vehicle while they looked for the remaining dog, but not too cold to cause problems.

"On the ATV?" Ava asked.

"Sure. The ATV gets around the pastures better than the truck."

"But how do we get the dog back if we find her?"

"One of us can walk back with her."

"Um," she said. "Okay."

The idea sounded solid until Ava climbed on the ATV behind him and wrapped her arms around his waist.

Immediately, his body hardened, and his heart somersaulted. He tightened his grip on the handlebars and forced his attention on the pasture ahead and not the sexy woman behind him. Except he could smell her gentle scent of soap and sunshine, and a deep longing caught him in the gut and twisted.

Why did she have to smell so darn good?

He drove slowly, scanning the pasture for any sign of the last missing dog. To his dismay and maybe yeah, secretly, to his delight, Ava rested her head against his back.

"Remember when you scored the winning touchdown during the homecoming game our junior year?" she asked.

That was a strange thing to bring up. He turned his head toward her, glancing over his shoulder to see the top of the helmet he'd given her to wear. "Yes. Why?"

"Because I think you may need to use some of that fancy footwork to capture Cinderella."

"Huh?"

She pointed.

There, running around in circles underneath a two-hundred-year-old oak tree, a dog barked at a chattering squirrel. The mutt was brown, yellow, black, and white. Cinderella looked to weigh about sixty pounds.

"That's some kind of focused attention," Caleb said, slowing the ATV. "She hasn't even glanced in our direction."

"Exactly. She will not surrender easily. She's fired up and could bolt on us. Something tells me she's the instigator of this whole escape. Cinderella's got the look of a runner."

Although tempted to growl, "takes one to know one," he didn't comment. The past was the past. Time to build a bridge and get over that water.

"Let the games begin," he said, stopping the ATV.

For the next ten minutes, they chased the dog around the trees. Cinderella thought it was a great game, even more interesting than treeing a squirrel, and gave them a run for their money. When Caleb came at the dog from one direction and Ava from another, Cinderella barked wildly and zigzagged between them.

She really was a wily thing, and if Caleb hadn't been trying to catch her, he would have admired the dog's agility. Seriously, Marjorie should enter her in agility training and teach her to come when called. Finally, out of breath, he stopped, racking his brain for a unique approach.

Ava jogged over to stand beside him and panted. "Cindy's a doozy." She was smiling and her face flushed prettily. She looked happy, radiant, and downright irresistible.

He nodded. They'd tried most every trick they could think of, but the dog still eluded them.

"What was it that Mr. Finster used to say in algebra class? The hardest problems to solve in life are the ones worth the most," Caleb said.

"I'm not sure about that, but Cinderella is a challenge."

"Should we warn Prince Charming?" he teased.

She laughed and murmured, "Gosh, I've missed you."

He'd missed her too. He almost told her, but before he could say a word, the dog darted straight toward him.

Now!

Instinctively, Caleb held his arms wide. If the dog got close enough, he was taking her down.

Cinderella leaped into the air and directly hit Caleb in the chest.

Oof.

Knocked to the ground, Caleb lay stunned. But somehow, he grabbed Cinderella's collar. He grunted, curled his fingers around the collar, and held on for all he was worth. The dog wriggled her hair and licked his face.

Ava ran over with the leash, clipped it to the

dog's collar, and pulled Cinderella off Caleb. "Are you okay?"

For a few moments, Caleb worked on getting air back into his lungs. It wasn't the first time he'd suffered a tackle, but man, he was older now, and it hurt more.

Finally, he sucked in a lungful of air and said, "F-fine."

"Are you sure?"

"Positive." He scrambled to his feet.

Ava continued to fuss over him, brushing straw from his clothes and inspecting him, while keeping a firm grip on Cinderella's leash. "Is anything hurt?"

"Other than my pride? No."

"You wouldn't keep the truth from me, would you?"

"I'm fine," he assured her.

"It really was just like that homecoming game," she said. "You got walloped hard."

"Yeah. It *was* like that."

He knew the game she meant. He'd been running down the field, his mind only half on what he was doing. Mostly he'd been thinking about Ava. She'd been flirting with him right before the game, waving her pom-poms in the air, the motion lifting her breasts beneath her cheerleader costume, and he was still playing her comments over in his mind when suddenly another player slammed into him.

The hit had knocked him flat. He'd redeemed himself later in the game by scoring two touchdowns, helping the team win the game. Ava had run onto the field despite being told to stand back. She took hold of his hand and refused to leave his side. Then she'd done something he hadn't expected.

She'd kissed him.

That night and her kiss were still in his mind as he took the dog from her and looped the leash around his hand. "Let me show you how to drive the ATV and I'll walk back with Cinderella."

"I've driven ATVs before. I can figure it out. You're the one I'm worried about. Are you sure you're okay?"

He nodded. "I'm fine, Ava. Stop fussing."

She grinned big. "I feel like I'm right back in high school."

"Well, except this time you're not wearing a hot little cheerleader uniform."

"I still own it." She winked. "Just saying."

Then before he could come up with an appropriate rejoinder, Ava went up on her tiptoes and kissed him.

CHAPTER 5

HAD SHE LOST HER MIND? Why on God's green earth had she kissed Caleb?

Maybe it was thinking back to the high school football game, or maybe it was watching him be such a good guy helping to round up her parents' unruly dogs.

Or maybe, if she were really honest with herself, it was because she simply *wanted* to kiss him. Had, in fact, wanted to kiss him ever since he'd held Buttons for Trudy Manfred at the photoshoot.

Caleb had always gotten under her skin, and not a thing had changed in that regard.

Frankly, she'd kissed him without thinking about it, not knowing if he would kiss her back. She'd shocked herself and assumed he'd pull away.

But he'd returned her kiss, had *really* kissed her. A deep kiss that made all the old feelings come flooding back.

She wasn't sure how long they'd stood next to his truck kissing, but eventually, the barking dogs inside the cab ended things.

Laughing, Caleb had glanced over at the dogs. Minnie Pearl, Oscar, Felix, and Cinderella had their faces pressed against the window, tongues lolling.

"We've put on quite a show," Caleb murmured, his arm draped loosely at her waist.

Ava laughed too, feeling thrilled. "Little snoops."

Caleb stepped back and nodded toward the truck. "Guess we'd better get these hooligans home."

He opened the passenger door for Ava, and once she settled inside, he circled around to the driver's side and climbed into the truck.

Silence rode with them.

She darted a glance at his handsome profile. What was he thinking? She fiddled with a button on the sleeve of her jacket and touched the tip of her tongue to her upper lip. "Are we going to talk about what just happened?"

He canted his head, slanted her a look, and shook his head. "Nope. I don't think we should."

"I see." She didn't see at all. She was desperate to know what was on his mind. "Why not?"

"Nothing to talk about. We hunted for dogs. We found dogs. We kissed. Now we're taking the dogs home. The end."

He didn't want to talk about it. Fine. She could shut down too.

"Okay." Pretending she was cool with that, Ava settled back in her seat and pretended she didn't give two hoots if he talked or not. What good would talking do, anyway? They were so different. It's not like they could ever be a couple again.

Right?

It was her fault. She shouldn't have kissed him. But, hey, at least he had kissed her back. That had been fun for a few minutes. Her mind conjured up a friends-with-benefits scenario, but she quickly shut those thoughts down.

Too scary.

Caleb pulled into the driveway and her parents came running out with Stephen King. Her mother opened the back of his pickup truck and released Minnie Pearl from her harness. "You found them all safe and sound. Thank heavens!"

"I'm sorry I forgot to lock the gate," her dad mumbled.

His mother leaned over to kiss his cheek. "It wasn't intentional. The dogs are safe. No harm, no foul."

"I've turned into a fumbling old fart." Dad jammed his hands into the pockets of his jeans and seemed lost.

Her dad looked so vulnerable it broke Ava's heart. She slung an arm around his shoulders. "You are no such thing. You've simply had too much on your plate. Anyone of any age could have forgotten to lock the gate."

"Want me to tell you some of the mistakes I've made over the years?" Caleb asked her father, but his eyes trained on Ava.

The heat of his gaze warmed her skin and Ava's heart fluttered. Oh dear, what was going on?

"Maybe sometime over a beer," her father said, grateful for Caleb's kindness. Ava was grateful as well. "I bet you've made a few doozies too."

Caleb nodded; his gaze locked on Ava. "Yep. Some pretty monumental ones."

"Thank you so much," her mother said. "We owe you big-time."

Caleb took off his Stetson and held it in his hands. "You don't owe me a thing. That's what friends and neighbors are for."

Friends.

He wasn't talking about her. He meant her parents and yet Ava had this crazy, wild hope that maybe, somehow, they could find their way back to each other.

Yeah? How's that going to happen when you're hardly ever here?

His head wasn't on his work and the horse knew it.

"Sorry, boy," he mumbled to one of the new horses he'd recently rescued as he brushed out his coat with a currycomb. "My mind's on a woman."

The horse, an aging gelding sorrel named Charger, had come to him missing his right eye and battling an infection from a barbed wire injury, but he was on the mend now. They had found Charger along with three other horses on an abandoned ranch in southwest Texas. Caleb had taken them all. Poor things. They deserved to live out the rest of their lives in safety and comfort with someone who loved them, and Caleb intended on supplying their needs to the end of their days.

"That's an enormous responsibility," said a voice behind him, almost as if reading his thoughts.

"You do know horses live twenty-five to thirty years."

Straightening, Caleb glanced up to see his rancher friend Zach Delaney standing in the stall's doorway. "I'm not going anywhere, and the new horses aren't colts."

Zach was grinning. "I've met no one less afraid of a commitment than you, Sutton, and I'm a third-generation rancher."

Caleb shrugged. "I know who I am. Why fight it? What's up, man?"

"I'm shopping for a horse for Abby Owens."

"Oh?" Caleb arched an eyebrow.

A telltale flush stained Zach's cheeks and his grin widened. "Suzannah and I are getting closer and—"

"Just how close?" Caleb wriggled his eyebrows.

"Get your mind out of the gutter. We're just great friends." Zach paused and then added with a wink. "For now."

"Hey, man, that's great. I've always thought you and Suzannah were good together."

"Speaking of getting closer," Zach said, jamming his hands into his pockets and kicking at the sawdust in Charger's stall. "How are things with you and Ava?"

"What do you mean?"

"Ava's back home since she's out of a job, and everyone's wondering if she's finally staying put for good."

"Ava's out of a job?"

"The company she was working for went out of business."

A strange and dangerous hope yanked on Caleb's heartstrings. Why should that excite him? Being jobless didn't scare Ava. She'd just find a new one. The woman had contacts all over the world. But yet, losing a job was a time for reflection, to reevaluate your life and see if...

Stop it.

"There's nothing between me and Ava."

"You sure?" Zach asked. "I saw some pretty sizzling looks pass between you two at the photoshoot the other day."

Caleb decided not to answer that. He just stared hard at his friend.

Zach took the hint. "Anyway, you got a gentle horse you might part with for Abby?"

Caleb nodded. "We can figure something out."

Zach studied Charger. "The gelding looks like he's doing a lot better."

Caleb patted the horse. "Time will tell, but I

think he'll be fine. Phil is doing an outstanding job with the horses. Thanks for recommending him."

"Glad I could help, but you're going to go bankrupt if you keep rescuing abandoned horses."

"Time will tell."

Zach had a point, but Caleb was sure he could turn things around for the horses who'd come to him in terrible shape. If he knew one thing, it was animals. He patted Charger and he nickered softly as if telling him he was grateful for the rescue.

"Besides, I get the horses for free and then love-struck ranchers like you show up wanting to buy one for kids who aren't even theirs—"

"Okay, okay." Zach chuckled. "You made your point. I won't argue with you. You know more about horses than I do. Heck, you know more about horses than anyone in Kringle, and I assume you know what you're doing with Ava."

"I'm not doing anything with her."

"That's my point."

"Excuse me?"

"When are you going to come to your senses and lasso that woman before she flits away again?"

"Why don't you take your own advice regarding Suzannah?"

"Hey, I'm working on it. Why do you think I'm here?"

"C'mon then." Caleb motioned for Zach to follow him. "I think I might just have the perfect horse for Abby."

———

Ava hadn't been to church since the last time she'd been in Kringle. She practiced a daily devotional, but it wasn't easy finding a regular church service to attend in her preferred denomination when she traveled all over the world and spent precious little time in any one place.

It felt nice being back home. Much nicer than she recalled.

Everyone greeted her as if they'd just been waiting for her to walk through the door. There were lots of hugs and handshakes and how-are-you-doings. The communion with the congregation felt familiar and natural and comforting. In her quest for adventure, she'd forgotten how comforting home and community and family could be.

She and her parents sat in their regular pew toward the front of the church, and she didn't even realize Caleb was there until the services were over and they turned to leave. She spied him standing at the back of the church talking to Zach, Suzannah, and Abby.

When his eyes met hers across the room, her heart and stomach did a funny little tango and she wanted to make a beeline straight for him, but Trudy Manfred stopped her.

"Ava, I loved the photos you sent me of Buttons and Thimble. You are such a gifted photographer."

"You're so welcome, Trudy. It was my pleasure."

"I wish you would move back to Kringle and become the town's official photographer."

Ava smiled indulgently at the older woman. Trudy was such a sweetheart.

"We wish that too," her mother said and put an arm around Ava's waist. "But her talent is simply too big for Kringle. Sadly, we have to share her with the world."

Ava crinkled her nose. Her mother's comment and the wistful tone in Mom's voice disturbed her. Was that how her mother really felt? Or was she just bragging a little to Trudy?

"Of course." Trudy sighed. "But if you ever do come back home, Ava, the town would support your photography business. Guaranteed."

"She knows," her mother said. "But the opportunity for growth just isn't here."

Oh my gosh, Ava thought. Her mother was using her own words against her. That was precisely what she'd told her parents when she announced she was leaving Kringle to make her way in the world as a photographer.

"I appreciate your kind words, Trudy."

"Give staying in Kringle some thought, Ava. We're more cosmopolitan than you might think. The internet has changed rural America. We're no longer hampered by small-town borders."

Trudy was so precious. Ava smiled. "Thank you for saying so."

"Kringle has an appeal that other places do not." Trudy glanced pointedly in Caleb's direction.

Uh-oh. Matchmaker alert!

"We have lots of nice things here." Trudy's grin lit up her eyes.

Caleb had finished up his conversation with Zach, Suzannah, and Abby and had come sauntering over, a sly smile on his face.

"Good morning, ladies. So..." He paused and settled his hands on his hips. "What 'nice things' are we discussing?"

"Nothing." Ava squirmed and didn't meet his steady gaze.

"It's nice that Ava's home for the holidays," her mother supplied.

"That it is." Caleb's rich voice wrapped around Ava like a welcoming hug. "Very nice for sure."

The look in Ava's eyes confirmed Caleb's suspicion. The three women had been talking about him.

Had Ava told her mother she'd kissed him? Somehow, he doubted it. Smiling, Caleb caught Ava's gaze, ran two fingers over his lips, and murmured, "It feels nice too."

Ava shot him a look that said, *please don't mention that we kissed.*

He widened his grin. She ought not to go around kissing men in a small town like Kringle if she worried her mama would find out.

But he wasn't looking to kick over that ant pile, so he let it go. Instead, he asked Marjorie, "How's Ted?"

"He's great. He's just over there talking to Roger Petri." Marjorie pointed.

Roger Petri was a real estate agent, and Caleb wondered if the conversation centered on putting the

Millers' house on the market. He shifted his gaze back to Ava, but he couldn't see any sign that she knew her parents planned on closing the shelter and moving into Kringle. He didn't believe it was right for her parents not to tell her what was going on, but he'd keep his mouth shut.

Stay out of it, Sutton. It's none of your business.

"Toodles." Trudy raised a hand goodbye. "I've got book club in an hour and need to put out snacks. Y'all have a good Sunday."

They said goodbye to Trudy, and Caleb set his Stetson back on his head since the church services were at an end.

"I was about to head for lunch at the Kringle Kafe," Caleb said. "Would the Millers care to join me?"

"That's such a sweet invitation," Marjorie said. "Thank you for asking, Caleb, but Ted and I have a thing. However, Ava's free."

It amused Caleb to see Ava narrow her eyes at her mother. "What kind of thing?"

"Now, now." Marjorie gave Caleb a look that said, *keep our secret.* "You know better than to ask too many questions near Christmastime. You don't want to ruin any surprises in the works."

To Caleb's way of thinking that was a weird

thing to say when the surprise Marjorie was hiding from Ava wasn't a pleasant one.

"Mom, what have you got up your sleeve?" Ava asked.

"Go, have a great lunch."

"I—"

"Your mother has spoken." Caleb tipped his hat to Marjorie and extended his arm to Ava, not really expecting her to take it, but she did and darn if he didn't thrill to it.

He led her outside. A few parishioners still gathered on the lawn chitchatting. It felt good having her on his arm, and he noticed more than a few heads turned to watch them. Ava was in heels, so he took the steps slowly, keeping a firm grip on her arm.

She sighed.

"What's that about?" he asked.

"You know Mom is getting ideas about us."

"She's not the only one. Zach Delaney stopped by to see me yesterday, and he was asking nosy questions about us."

"Uh-oh. Zach is the least gossipy person in town besides you. If he's in on this, we're in trouble."

He shrugged. "Small excitement in a small town. People love a wonderful story of high school sweethearts reunited. It gives them something to talk about."

Ava disengaged from his arm, turned, and looked at him. She was standing so close that he could see the sprinkle of freckles across the bridge of her nose.

Ducking her head to hide a pink flush staining her cheeks, she said, "I guess everyone thinks we're getting back together."

"They can think what they like. We know the truth."

"Have people been warning you against me?"

"Something like that."

"Really?" She sighed again. "I'm so very sorry for hurting you. I was young and thoughtless."

It surprised Caleb that she'd brought it up. He figured they'd leave the past buried as they had every other time she'd come home. For a second, he considered telling her that she hadn't hurt him, but then he was truthful.

"I know you didn't mean to do it," he said in the kindest voice he could muster. "I know you had to do what was right for you. It was unfair of me to expect you to be on board without considering what was best for us both."

Her eyes glistened in the sunlight. "Thank you for saying that. For being so understanding. I didn't mean to hurt you. I really didn't. At eighteen, I was eager and wide-eyed. There was so much I wanted to do in life. I felt like I couldn't achieve my dreams if I stayed here. My genuine mistake was getting too close to you. I knew I needed more than Kringle could offer and I also knew you were a man anchored in Kringle soil."

Ouch. Was she unintentionally calling him a stick-in-the-mud?

"You did what you felt you needed to do. I understand and I got over it. And for the record, the joy of being with you, even for just a few years, was worth any pain, Ava."

Her mouth turned down and her eyes looked so sad. "It's better to have loved and lost than never to have loved at all?"

"Something like that."

"Why did you kiss me back the other day?"

Her question caught him off guard. Truthfully, he wasn't sure how he wanted things to go with Ava, but he knew one thing. He was still deeply attracted to her.

"I wanted to." That was as much of an answer as he had.

"Should I apologize for kissing you?" She flipped a strand of hair over her shoulder and shifted her weight, rocking on the balls of her feet, her high heels grinding slightly on the concrete sidewalk.

He readjusted his Stetson and studied her. "No, but for the record, I read nothing into your kiss. I understand that you're impulsive. I know it means nothing."

Her face scrunched up and her voice wavered. "It doesn't?"

"Does it?" He wasn't sure what response he'd expected from her, but it wasn't the one he got. He would have thought the last thing she'd want was to get involved with him again.

"Do you think that maybe...we could..." She cleared her throat and curled the fingers of both hands into her palms.

"Pick up where we left off?"

Her eyes widened and she nodded.

"I haven't changed," he told her. "I still love Kringle. I like being settled. I like the town, the community, the people. I have everything I need right here."

"Everything?" she asked.

He eyed her. "Well, maybe not *everything*, but I'm only twenty-eight. I still have plenty of time to find love, get married, and raise a family."

"I'm the one who's changed," she said. "I realize now what I threw away."

"I'm glad for your personal growth." It took everything he had in him not to whisk her into his arms, kiss her for all he was worth, and tell her he'd just been waiting for her to wake up and realized where she belonged.

In Kringle.

With him.

But he couldn't do that and not just because a good percentage of the church's patronage was staring at them.

Caleb ached to believe that she'd changed and that she was sincere. But deep down, he wasn't sure. The only thing he *was* sure about was that he'd never gotten over Ava Miller and he wasn't sure he ever would.

A small, soft smile crossed her sexy lips. She reached over to caress his face. "Question is cowboy, what do *you* want?"

"I want to go to lunch with you, Ava Miller."

And so they did.

CHAPTER 6

ONCE THEY SETTLED into a back booth at the Kringle Kafe, Ava gave a jaunty wave to people she knew—which was most everyone.

The place had changed little over the years. The color scheme was new, and it looked like they'd reupholstered a few of the booths, but mostly, it was the same as it had always been—gossip central.

"Hey, this is just like old times," Sandy, the waitress, said as she handed them menus. "Caleb and Ava together again."

Ava's pulse skipped. Oh dear, coming here was clearly a mistake. They were stoking the rumor mill. She'd been away too long if she'd forgotten the blinding speed of the Kringle grapevine.

After Sandy took their orders and walked away,

Caleb looked across the table at Ava and raised one bemused eyebrow. "How long do you think it will take for news of this meal to saturate the town? An hour? Two tops?"

She laughed. "I suspect most everyone will know what we ate before we even start eating it."

Caleb swept off his Stetson and settled it into the bottom of the chair beside him. "Does it bother you? We could leave."

"I have nothing to be ashamed of. I'm having lunch with my neighbor; what's wrong with that?"

"A neighbor who was once your high school sweetheart."

"Granted." She grinned.

"A neighbor whom you broke up with the day before the wedding." His tone was mild, to show he wasn't holding a grudge.

"Better than the day after." She rested both palms on the table, her menu between the frame of her hands, and listened to the sound of her blood whooshing through her ears. She was so sharply aware of him—his wry smile, his heavenly masculine scent, the way his gray eyes missed nothing.

Caleb nodded. "Yep. Nothing around here has changed."

Canting her head, she studied him. "That's not true. *You've* changed."

"You think? How's that?"

Ava rubbed two fingers over her chin. "You're more relaxed. More self-confident."

"I haven't changed," he reiterated, leaning back in his chair. "The only thing that's changed is your perception of me."

Was that true? This time, her heart skipped two beats.

"No, really," he said. "I'm serious. I'm the same guy I was when we were in high school. I still work the ranch all day. I still love where I live and have no desire to move. I still order the same thing at the Kringle Kafe no matter who's with me."

Ava laughed. He was right. He had ordered the same chicken fried steak he'd always ordered when they'd been dating in high school. "Okay, so maybe you haven't changed all that much."

With a nonchalant shrug, he added, "No reason to change if you're happy with who you are."

Sandy arrived to deposit their food in front of them. She told them to enjoy and wandered off again.

"I guess that's where we're different. I like trying new things and crave new experiences."

"You always want something new and different. I get it. You like keeping your options open. Me? When I find what I like, I stick with it. I'm more closed-ended."

Closed off is more like it.

He held her gaze for a powerful moment, and she felt that stare right down to her toes. He'd always had a startling effect on her, and it seemed the strength of it hadn't dimmed over the years. She thought he might say something else, but he merely cleared his throat and glanced away.

Leaving Ava feeling bizarrely bereft.

He picked up his knife and fork and went after his chicken fried steak, so she turned her attention to her food too. She'd ordered the cashew chicken salad, but now, piercing at the wilted iceberg lettuce with the tines of her fork, she couldn't help wishing she'd ordered the chili mac instead.

"You should have ordered the chili mac," Caleb said, reading her mind.

She laughed softly. "You think you're so smart. I *wanted* a salad."

He shook his head. "I don't think so. I think you wanted chili mac, but you ordered the cashew chicken salad because it's new on the menu and you wanted to try something different, even though secretly you yearned for your old standby."

"You're wrong." She took a bite, hoping to prove him incorrect, but she knew in her heart he was correct. She *loved* the chili mac at the Kringle Kafe. Nothing else compared.

"Admit it, chili mac is your first culinary crush."

She met Caleb's eyes. "We're not talking about food anymore, are we?"

"It's a metaphor." He shrugged.

"Meaning you're the chili mac and I keep chasing after cashew chicken salad?"

"Your words, not mine." He cut into his chicken fried steak, stuck a bite in his mouth, and chewed. "Mmm."

She mimicked him, taking a big bite of her salad, moaning "mmm" and patting her belly.

Caleb flagged down Sandy.

"What is it, dollface?" Sandy asked.

"Could you bring Ava a bowl of chili mac instead?" Caleb asked.

"On it." Sandy saluted him. "That cashew chicken salad is on the menu for the tourists. Everyone in Kringle knows to order the chicken fried steak or chili mac when they walk through those doors. I figured Ava's been gone so long, she forgot."

Ava pushed her plate to one side. With the promise of chili mac, she was over the salad.

"Tell me about your travels," Caleb invited after Sandy went to place the new order.

"Do you really want to know?"

"I want to know everything about the woman you've become," he said. From the rapt way he gave her his attention, she believed he meant it.

"I'm not sure where to start. I know my parents have kept you updated on my travels."

"Not as much as you might think. How many countries have you visited?" Caleb asked.

"Oh, wow, I've lost count." She touched the tip of her tongue to her upper lip, then looked up and to the right as she ticked off countries on her fingers. "France, Spain, Italy, Germany, most of Europe really. I've been to the Netherlands and Norway, Slovenia and Croatia. The Czech Republic, Poland, Austria, Switzerland. Ack! Look, I'm out of fingers and I haven't even gotten started with the South Pacific and Asia."

"You've been a busy woman."

"How about you? How many countries did you visit when your dad was in the military?"

"Not as many as you and I went to twelve different schools."

"Don't you ever miss it?" she asked. "Traveling around the world?"

"It was never like that for me," he said. "Traveling isn't something I did for fun. It was my dad's job and I got dragged along. I'm not blaming my dad. That was his livelihood and for sure, I learned a lot. Mostly, that I'm the kind of guy who enjoys staying in one place."

Here they were, back to the same old conflict. He craved certainty. It was a yolk around her neck.

At least it had been ten years ago.

Here? Now? With her last job ended and nothing new on the horizon, maybe she was tired of starting over every few months. Staying on the move might fill her life with adventure, but it stopped her from establishing the comforting rhythm of a steady routine.

"I remember when you got on that plane to Paris, on what was supposedly our wedding day, with nothing more than your five thousand dollars in your bank account and a place to stay." Caleb shook his head. "I couldn't believe how brave you were. Your pluck amazes me."

"Really?" She laid her fork down on her plate and met his gaze. "You thought I was brave?"

He gave a slow, solemn nod. "So damn brave."

"Why didn't you ever tell me?"

"I was selfish." He lifted a shoulder. "And feeling petty that Paris got you and not me."

"Aww, Caleb."

He raised a palm. "No pity. You did what you had to do, and I had to learn how to let you do it."

"You know," she said, "that's one of the most understanding things you've ever said to me."

"Hey, don't canonize me. It took me ten years to get here."

"Me as well."

"What happened when you got to Paris with no job prospects? How did you plan to survive?"

"It's probably braggy of me to say so, but I really didn't worry. I knew I was a talented photographer and I didn't mind scrimping to get by. I vowed to follow the river of life where it took me."

He grimaced.

"Too New-Agey for Kringle?" She laughed.

"Not at all. I just couldn't do something like that. It's important to me to always have a plan."

"I know." Her smile gentled. "You crave certainty and I crave adventure."

"Not a compatible combo, is it?"

"I dunno. I've always heard opposites attract."

"Walk me through what happened. You're just

off the plane at Orly. You're wandering through Paris. What happened next?"

"I met a newlywed American couple on the bus to the pension and we got to chatting and I told them how I'd left you behind to follow my bliss. They hired me to photograph their honeymoon travel throughout Europe. It was a total blast. I thought they were poor like me because they were staying in a pension, but I found out they were just being frugal, saving their money for a startup company. They hired me to do freelance photography and graphic design. I still work for them occasionally."

"I swear, Ava," he said, admiration in the respectful shake of his head. "No matter what happens, you always come out smelling like a rose."

"Not always. The stories I could tell you about my missteps." Laughing, she tossed her head. "But mistakes are how we learn, right?"

"Right," Caleb echoed.

Sandy returned with the chili mac. "Hey, Ava, what do you think of Caleb's remodeled kitchen?"

Ava knew a fishing expedition when she heard one. Sandy was looking for juicy gossip. Ava looked across the table at Caleb. "You remodeled your kitchen?"

"Yep."

Sandy looked disappointed that Ava hadn't known and added, "All by himself."

"Not all by myself. I had help from Phil and Mort."

"Not *professional* help. Get him to show you pictures. I'll be back to check on you soon." Sandy picked up Ava's abandoned salad.

"Thank you," Ava said to Sandy, To Caleb, she said, "I want to see pics."

"Of...?"

"Your remodel." She motioned for him to call up the photographs on his phone while Sandy moved on to the next table.

"These pictures aren't up to Ava Miller standards," he said, taking his phone from his jacket pocket.

"*Please.* I'll be looking at your remodeling skills, not your photography talent."

Grinning, Caleb handed over his cell phone.

Making the pictures bigger on the phone screen, Ava studied the changes in the old farmhouse kitchen. She'd always loved Caleb's home, especially the big sprawling kitchen. But nothing looked the same. Gone was the dark brown and yellow color scheme she remembered. Now the kitchen gleamed with stainless steel appliances and black quartz countertops. Modern white cabinets replaced the dark oak. Even the floor was new, with a gray herringbone patterned tile.

"Wow, you really remodeled."

"Yes, my ranch hands, Phil and Mort, are also good with construction. We did the remodeling over a few weekends last winter."

She studied the picture, admiring their handiwork. The room was modern and bright. Ava couldn't help feeling a little sad that the old kitchen was gone, but they'd done an excellent job. "I'm impressed."

"Why? You know I like to putter."

Only Caleb would consider a massive kitchen remodel "puttering." The man was the salt of the earth—solid, dependable, an all-round reliable guy.

And she'd missed him more than she'd realized.

"I'm just surprised by your skills," she said. "I had no idea you were so accomplished at construction."

He laughed. "A little remodeling job hardly counts as construction. Plus, Phil and Mort have both worked in building maintenance. What we didn't know, we learned on YouTube. I'm pretty proud of us."

"You should be." She passed the phone back to

him. "That's excellent work. If you ever gave up ranching, you could always fall back on flipping houses."

"It *was* fun. I wish you could have been there."

"Me too," she said and meant it.

"You have a brilliant eye for detail and design," Caleb said. "You've come a long way."

She studied him. "We really are different people now than we were ten years ago, aren't we?"

"Why? Just because I successfully remodeled a kitchen?" He set down his fork and knife and blinked at her.

"No. It's much more than that."

"Oh?"

"You're much more open than you used to be."

"Am I?"

"Although you still serve up the same monosyllables." She smiled at him. "But I see some expansion."

"How's that?"

"You're willing to give me another chance."

"Is that what I'm doing?"

"You invited me to dine with you at the Kringle Kafe at noon on a Sunday in full view of devoted churchgoers, so yes, that's how I'm interpreting it."

"For the record, I invited your parents too."

"That was your safety net."

"And still when the safety net bailed, I brought you anyway," he mused and seemed surprised by the thought. "Maybe I will give you a second chance, if you wanted one."

"After the way I left things?" She dabbed chili mac from her bottom lip. "I didn't know if you'd ever even speak to me again."

"I was hurt, I admit it. And I sulked. Not proud of it, but not ashamed either. A guy's got to get through losing his first love anyway he can."

First love.

Ava's heart quickened. "I'm so sorry for what I put you through."

"I'm not. You found yourself. And me? Well, I learned not to take *anything* for granted."

Her heart broke right in two. "Oh, Caleb."

They sat there, gazes locked over chicken fried steak and chili mac. Being here with him at Christmastime felt perfect.

"May I ask you something?" She took a drink of water.

"Sure, but I can't promise I'll answer."

"Fair enough."

"How come you haven't gotten married by now? Why don't you have a passel of kids? That's the life you were made for, Cabe. Home, family, the whole nine yards."

His measured gaze never left her face. She felt the heat on her cheeks. "I did date after you. A lot, in fact, but I couldn't find anyone that compared."

"That's silly. There're tons of wonderful women in Kringle. What about Suzannah Owens?"

"She's Zach's girl."

"Chloe?"

"We never got to a third date."

"You dated Chloe? I didn't know that."

"We drove to Fort Worth for our dates to dodge the rumor mill."

"Why didn't it work? You're both terrific people."

Caleb's eyes drilled Ava to her seat. "Nothing. We just didn't have chemistry. Chloe is a wonderful woman and she's a great friend, but...she's not *you*."

That took her breath away, and Ava abandoned her beloved chili mac completely.

"Zach told me the company you were working for went out of business. Do you have another job lined up?"

Ava was finding it increasingly hard to breathe deeply. "No."

"I see. But you'll find another job soon."

"No doubt."

"Forever footloose and fancy free," his eyes and voice softened.

"Forever," she echoed.

"The thing I love most about you is the thing that pulls you away from me," he murmured.

Love. He'd said the word love in connection with her? Could Caleb possibly still love her after all these years? After she'd broken his heart so badly? She felt like a prisoner who'd gotten an unexpected parole.

He took a deep breath, held it, then exhaled slowly. "I suppose there's a part of me that always hoped you'd return home for good."

"I'm not planning on staying in Kringle, Caleb."

"I know," he said, and he looked so sad it shattered Ava's spirit. "But I'm okay with a long-distance relationship if that's what it takes to hold on to you."

Literally, he could have knocked her over with an ostrich feather if he'd had one.

"Y-you'd be open to that?"

He reached across the table and took her hand. "For the first time in ten years, I think we're finally on the same page. Neither one of us is dating anyone else. We're both willing to give each other space to be who we truly need to be."

"I-I don't know what to say." *Say nothing. Do a happy dance.* Stunned by the development, she did nothing.

"Let's not say anything. Let's just enjoy being together."

"And feeding the rumor mill." Ava chuckled and nodded at Sandy, who was surreptitiously taking a picture of them with the cell phone she'd pulled from her pocket.

"It gives the town gossips a thrill."

"So, we're dating?"

"Let's not label anything beyond a fresh start."

"Fresh start?"

"Fresh start."

She jumped from her side of the booth and landed on his side of the table and extended her hand with a grin as wide as his own. "It's nice to meet you, Caleb Sutton."

Caleb shook it and tugged her closer. "It's nice to meet you too, Ava Miller."

It was such a lovely moment, but to appreciate it, Ava had to shove aside the niggling voice at the back of her brain that whispered, *now where do you go from here?*

CHAPTER 7

"WHAT ARE YOU DOING AFTER THIS?" Caleb asked as he left two twenties on the table to cover their bill and a twenty-five percent tip for Sandy.

"I'm plastering downtown in Home for the Holidays posters. I've already gotten permission from town hall. Wanna help?"

"Absolutely." He settled his Stetson on his head and led the way to the front door.

"Great. Let's go get the flyers from my car." She headed toward her parents' second car that she borrowed whenever she came to visit.

"First things first." Caleb took her elbow.

"Where are we going?" she asked, delighted by a surprise. She *loved* surprises.

He tugged her into the alleyway, out of sight from passersby. "Here."

She glanced around at the cobblestone path leading behind the buildings. They were alone. "Why?"

"This."

Without another word, Caleb pushed his cowboy hat back on his head, gathered Ava into his arms, and kissed her.

He kissed her just like he had in the old days, hot and passionate, except with more confidence and experience. It was the kind of kiss that made her toes curl and her mind go blank to anything and everything except the feel of his lips on hers.

She sank against his chest, absorbing his heat, her entire body coming alive beneath his lips. Oh, how she'd missed kissing him!

They kissed and kissed and kissed and she felt sixteen all over again and madly in love for the very first time.

At last, he tenderly pulled back and smiled down at her.

"Wow," she whispered, fingering her lips. "That was some kiss."

His grin expanded. "It was some kind of kiss."

Her gaze searched his, and she saw a gentle light in his eyes that yanked on her heartstrings and sent her mind whirling. *What if?*

What if she gave up roaming? What if she came home for good? What if she and Caleb…?

"Is it as good as you remembered?" he asked.

"Fishing for compliments, Sutton? That's not your style." She laughed and lowered her voice. "But for the record? The years have refined your kissing technique."

"I do my best to stay up on all the new kissing techniques," he said. "It's a global world these days."

"That it is." She dusted her palms together, trying to disperse her gathering desire for him. This development was new and fantastic, but it had scary consequences she wasn't ready to deal with. "Let's go put up those posters."

"Let's do it." He offered his arm and she took it without hesitation, aching to be as close to him as she could.

They went to her car and got out the posters. Ava divided the stack and gave half to Caleb.

He studied them. "This is a terrific poster."

"Thank you." She beamed.

"The event is going to be outstanding with you at the helm and the shelter really needs clearing out."

"That's so nice of you to say."

"You inherited your parents' passion for helping." He paused and a faraway look came into his eyes.

"What is it?" she prodded.

He shook himself and blinked. "Could I offer a small suggestion about the event? I know you don't like to plan. I honor your process, but I do fret."

Ava cloaked a smile. He was looking after her. That was so sweet. When they'd dated, he always planned and scheduled everything. Ava appreciated his concern, but she wished he wouldn't worry so much. She knew he liked to plan things down to the last detail, and in fact, more than once when they'd been young, his need to overthink situations had caused disagreements.

Although, to be fair, not any more than her tendency to follow her whims had.

She liked to go with the flow, to see where the moment took her and not plan out every detail. Being spontaneous made life more exciting, but she knew it made Caleb uncomfortable.

Some people in town believed she'd thoughtlessly stomped on Caleb's heart and cavalierly took off for Europe. But it hadn't been like that. She'd begged him to come with her. Caleb was the one who said no. He was the one who'd told her to go off and find herself.

And she had.

"Worrywart," she teased. "What's on your mind?"

"Have you thought about crowd control?"

"Crowd control?"

"In case you draw in a lot of potential adopters."

"This is Kringle."

"And this..." He held up the posters. "Is attention grabbing. You could have people coming from Fort Worth and beyond."

"You think?"

"It doesn't hurt to think about crowd control. The interior front office in the shelter is a ten-by-fourteen-foot space. Get six people in there and you have a crowd."

He made a good point.

"I'll take your concerns under advisement, but I'm sure it will be fine. I have a few volunteers coming over that day, and I'm sure we can handle whatever mad mob descends." She couldn't suppress her smile.

"Don't laugh," he said. "I'm serious. It's better to be overprepared than underprepared."

"Caleb, I really don't think crowd control will be a problem. Finding suitable homes for shelter pets has always been a challenge."

"You never know. Your posters could change all that. People may flock to adopt a pet."

"We should be so lucky. Speaking of posters, let's go hang these and see if we can't rustle up the need for crowd control."

Caleb grinned and shook his head. "Okay, but I still say you need to plan for overflow."

"Fine, fine, you win. I surrender. What do you suggest?"

"First, mark off a perimeter in the field around the shelter for extra space for parking."

"Done. I'll get on that as soon as I return home."

"I can get one of my ranch hands to spray paint the grass where visitors are allowed to park if that helps."

"Good idea. Sure. I'll take all the help I can get."

Ava thought about the small parking lot in front of the shelter. She'd never really considered it before, but the three parking spaces were pretty limited. Rarely did they have more than one or two potential adopters at a time, so they'd needed nothing bigger.

Caleb had a point. If even a few more cars showed up, there would be no place to park.

She tapped her chin. "You might be right. We need additional parking."

To his credit, Caleb didn't gloat, although she suspected he wanted to.

"Go ahead. Admit it," she said, tucking the posters under her arm and hitting the 'lock' button on her car remote.

He backed out of the parking space and headed toward Kringle. "Admit what?"

"You were right, and I was wrong."

"It's not about right and wrong, Ava. It's about having an effective event. That's all I want. I'm not trying to tell you how to run your business."

"Good." She grinned.

They headed down the sidewalk together, a comfortable silence settling between them.

Caleb was one of the few people she could spend a chunk of time with and not feel compelled to chatter. His presence calmed her. Not only was she sexually attracted to him, but she genuinely liked him as a person, and she enjoyed being around him. He was the salt of the earth. A man you could count on.

She stopped at the crosswalk on the corner.

She pulled a staple gun and a roll of heavy-duty

tape from her purse. "Which one do you want? Take your pick."

"Look at you." He laughed. "Planning ahead."

"Watch out, Sutton," she teased, shaking the tape roll in his face. "I'm not the same sweet little girl I was ten years ago."

"You were never sweet."

"Point made." She waggled her head from side to side and sent him a comical grin.

He burst out laughing. "Heavens above, Ava," he said, surprising them both. "I've missed you."

Oh, Caleb, I've missed you too!

Since Kringle's downtown wasn't that big, it didn't take long for them to work their way around the town square. All the local businesses that opened on Sunday agreed to let her put a poster in their windows. Ava noticed how store owners would eye her, then Caleb, and look back at her again. No one came right out and asked if they were a couple, but she knew the question lay on tips of tongues.

Caleb went into the ice cream parlor to put up a sign while Ava ambled through the door of the bakery, Kringle Kakes. The owner, Mike Honeycutt, greeted her with a great big smile. Mike had known both her and Caleb in high school, although he'd been a couple of years behind them.

"Hey, Ava, are you here to order a wedding cake?" Trust class clown Mike to be the first one to make a joke.

"Nooo," she said. "I was thinking of ordering a funeral cake for you if you keep up this line of questioning."

He laughed again. "I'm just messin' with you."

Ava stood in the middle of the bakery, holding the posters, her thoughts a jumbled mess. Marriage? To Caleb? She hadn't been looking that far into the future. Marriage talk gave her the heebie-jeebies. Sure, she was glad to see Caleb again, and heartened that they were working through their past issues. She definitely wanted to date him. But marriage?

Well, that just felt too darn nice, didn't it?

"Um, do you mind if I hang this poster in your window? It's for an adoption event we're having the day after the parade."

"Home for the Holidays, I heard." Mike grinned and wiped his hands on a kitchen towel. "Sure thing. Happy to help."

She placed the sign in the window and headed for the door.

"Let me know when you want to put down a deposit on a wedding cake," Mike called.

"You'll be the last to know." She chuckled to

show she wasn't the least bit thrown by his ribbing. "Thank you for letting me hang the poster."

"No problem, Mrs. Sutton." Mike chortled.

As the cowbell over the door jangled, Ava groaned. *Welcome home to Kringle.*

"Guess what," she told Caleb when they reconvened at her car.

"What?"

"Apparently, we're getting married."

"No kidding." He pushed his Stetson back on his forehead and propped the toe of his boot on the curb. "First I'm hearing of it."

"Me too."

He shook his head. "This town. You gotta love it."

"All kidding aside," Ava said. "We can't let this town run our lives."

"I agree completely."

"I'm happy being home. Whenever you come into the room, I feel lighter, safer, but at the moment, I'm not interested in anything more than dating. Is that all right with you?"

He just looked at her for a long moment, and then said, "My thoughts precisely."

"You agree?"

"We shouldn't jump into anything. Let's take

things nice and slow. Test the waters. See if we really want to flame the embers."

"Yes, yes, slow, slow," she said, but her throat was scratchy, and her chest felt tight. Was she coming down with a cold?

Or could it be she was actually more into Caleb than he was into her?

"Hey," he said. "I just remembered I have a can of orange spray paint in the back of my truck. What say I follow you back to the rescue and mark off the extra parking spots so that's one more thing off your plate."

"What?" she teased. "You don't trust me to handle it?"

"Just an offer." His shrug was casual, but the heat in his eyes was anything but.

"To go out your way for me? Why?"

"Peanut," he said with complete sincerity. "I'd go to the ends of the earth for you."

———

Caleb guided his truck behind Ava's compact as they headed back to the rescue.

Something had changed with Ava while they'd been hanging up posters. Based on his own experience, he'd be willing to bet that people in town had asked her about them as a couple.

It had freaked her out a little. Heck, it had freaked him out a little too. It had devastated him when she'd broken off their engagement, and he really didn't want to go through that again.

But dang, he wanted to try.

Just as Ava pulled to a stop at her parents' house, the door to the shelter opened and a panicked-looking young man with a ponytail came running out, flagging Ava down. Caleb recognized him as one of the shelter volunteers, Devon Crocket.

He parked, got out, and ambled over to where Devon waited for Ava to emerge from her car. Caleb watched her in the afternoon's glow, admiring the way her hair curled around her shoulders. She had such beautiful hair, and his fingers itched to run through the silky stands.

Now that he was closer, Caleb could see that Devon held a tiny Chihuahua in the crook of his arm.

"Your parents aren't home from church yet, and I'm panicking!" Devon exclaimed. "Juliet threw up several times. I think she might have swallowed a bug," he said. "There are bug guts in her cage."

Ava took the Chihuahua from him. "Do you know what kind of bug it was?"

The young man shook his head. "I didn't see it when it was alive. I only noticed what she left of it when I went to feed her. Ick! There're body parts strewn all over her cage." Devon shuddered. "I guess I'll have to clean it up."

How big was this darn bug? Caleb wondered. Devon was prone to overexaggeration.

"I hope it wasn't poisonous," Ava fretted. "Ladybugs can cause ulcers in dogs and—"

Devon shook his head. "It was way too big for a ladybug. Those guts are *everywhere*."

The kid made it sound like a crime scene.

"Stink bugs can cause gastrointestinal distress—"

"Eew! Eew!" Devon slapped his palms over his ears.

The young man was a bit of a drama king. Caleb nipped this ridiculous guessing game in the bud.

"I'll go inspect the bug guts," Caleb offered. "And clean up the mess."

Devon pressed his palms together in front of his heart. "Oh, thank you, thank you, thank you."

Ava rubbed the Chihuahua's head. "So, little missy, why did you eat a bug?"

Caleb chuckled. The little dog was wagging her

tail and looked as happy as could be, and she leaned up to give Ava puppy kisses.

Ava dodged the dog's tongue. "No, little lady. You're not allowed to kiss me with bug lips."

"Good to know," Caleb said.

The dog seemed fine now to him. When he went back to the Chihuahua's pen, he found click beetle viscera. Juliet had had a high old time tearing the insect to bits. The mess was trivial, and Caleb cleaned it up in one swipe with an antibacterial wipe. The other dogs had barked their heads off as soon as he'd come in.

"You guys make a good alarm," he told them as he headed to the office. "Too bad you weren't able to scare away the bug."

Devon and Ava were in the office. Ava had plopped down on the couch while Devon paced the small space.

"Look who is already feeling great!" Ava waved at the Chihuahua scampering around without a care.

Caleb laughed and sat next to Ava. Their knees touched and she didn't move her leg away.

Juliet jumped into Caleb's lap and gave a fierce little yap that said, *pay attention to me*.

"Juliet, it's nice to meet you. I just cleaned up what you left of the bug. A thank you is in order."

Juliet plunked down on his thigh and sized him up. She must have decided she liked what she saw because she curled right up and closed her eyes.

"What kind of bug was it?" Ava asked. "Cockroaches carry intestinal parasites. If it was a cockroach, I should take Juliet in to see Chloe."

"It was a click beetle, and I think little of it ended up inside her. But she went to sleep really quickly. Now I'm wondering if fatigue is a sign of click beetle poisoning." Caleb was kidding, but Ava seemed to think he was being serious.

"Mom says she does that. Juliet's got narcolepsy. She can fall asleep standing up at her food dish."

"No kidding? Dogs get narcolepsy?" Caleb raised an eyebrow. "Who knew? Juliet's unique."

At the sound of her name, Juliet woke from her nap and hopped to her feet, her tail wagging so fast Caleb feared she'd fall right over.

"She looks pretty healthy now," he said.

"I'm sure she'll be fine now that we know it was a click beetle, but I'll take her to the house so I can keep a close eye on her. This isn't the first time a dog ate a bug at our shelter. I'm sure it won't be the last. It happens."

"I ate a bug once," Caleb blurted, surprising himself with his confession.

"What? On purpose? Like eating gourmet insects?"

He laughed at her horrified expression. "Not on purpose. When I was eight and on a camping trip with the Boy Scouts, a bug flew into my mouth."

Ava brought a hand to her throat and made gagging noises.

"Hey, stuff happens."

Grinning, Ava leaned away from him. "Ick."

He nodded slowly. "Yep, I agree now—*ick*. But it gave me a cool rep with the rest of the Scout pack. They even gave me a nickname."

"Dare I ask?" She laughed and patted him on the arm.

"You sure you want to know?"

"Why not?"

"It might turn you off of me for good."

"How bad can it be?"

"Fly Slayer."

"Eww!"

"C'mon, baby, pucker up. Wanna kiss the Fly Slayer?"

Laughing, she put a palm to his chest to hold him at bay. "I am not interested in kissing the Fly Slayer. Now, Caleb Sutton is a whole other matter."

"You wouldn't let Juliet kiss you with her bug lips. Why the change of heart?" he teased.

"Your bug incident was twenty years ago. I trust you've brushed your teeth since then."

"I've even got peppermints." He pulled two pieces of candy from his pocket. "Want one?"

"Sure." She took the peppermint from him, unwrapped it, and popped it into her mouth.

He did the same, sucking on the candy.

She chomped hers.

He'd forgotten how impatient she was, always in a hurry to get to the good stuff while Caleb believed half the fun was in the anticipation.

"C'mon," she said. "I'll walk you to your truck." To Devon, she said, "Keep an eye on Juliet for me, please."

The young man took the Chihuahua and Ava led Caleb outside.

At his truck, he paused and looked down at her.

She pursed her lips.

This peppermint-flavored kiss was even better than the one before. She wrapped her arms around his neck and pulled him closer.

Her lips sent his entire body to tingling. How he wanted to keep kissing her for endless hours until their lips turned cracked and raw, but they'd agreed to take things slowly, because long-distance relation-ships were tricky, and he was a man who prided himself on sticking to his guns.

With as much self-control as he could muster, he broke the kiss. "I gonna head on out. Text or call me if you need anything."

"Thanks for lunch and helping me pass out the posters and for your clear-eyed thinking in the click beetle crisis. It was nice having you here. You've got a calming energy."

"I don't know about that," he mused.

"I do. I've been alone for so long I'd forgotten how nice it was to have a sidekick."

"Is that what I am?" He searched her face and saw a longing in her eyes that matched his own.

"I hope you're my friend."

"I am," he said. "Always."

She leaned in for one more quick kiss. "Bye-bye, Fly Slayer."

"I'm never going to hear the end of that, am I?"

"Not on your life," she teased.

"See if I tell you any more of my deep, dark secrets."

"As if you have any."

"Don't laugh," he said. "You've been away for ten years. You have no idea what I've been up to behind your back." Then, with a quick kiss on her cheek and a wink, he closed the door behind him and drove away.

It wasn't until he got home that Caleb realized he'd forgotten to use the orange paint to spray off a parking area for her in the field.

CHAPTER 8

ON MONDAY MORNING, Ava was partway up the ladder at Caleb's house when he walked out of the barn, headed for his tractor.

He stopped and sank his hands onto his hips, widening his stance.

She waved at him, unsurprised when he abandoned his mission to head her way. He looked grumpy, but she had to admit, even scowling, he was handsome as all get-out.

"What are you doing?" he asked.

"Surprise! We're decorating," she said, nodding toward the string of Christmas lights in her hands. "What are you doing?"

Two men wandered from the barn behind Caleb. Ava assumed they were his ranch hands, Phil and

Mort. She glanced down at Devon, who was holding the ladder for her. Today, his hair was pulled back in a tidy man-bun.

"You remember Devon." She nodded.

"Hi," Caleb said to Devon. To Ava, he said, "That's dangerous."

"Robert brought the ladder," she said with a blithe smile.

"What's that got to do with the price of tea in China?" Caleb's scowl deepened.

"Huh?" Confused, Devon scratched his head.

"Keep your hands on the ladder at all times, kid." Caleb grabbed hold of the ladder. "That's precious cargo on those rungs."

Aww! That was a sweet thing to say.

"Robert's a house painter, so he buys top quality ladders," Ava explained. "Nothing to worry about."

"You should have scaffolding."

"Oh, Robert brought that too." She pointed to a white panel truck parked in his driveway, where Robert, a close friend of her parents, was unloading scaffolding. His wife Lisa was there, too, taking bags of Christmas decorations from the back seat. "That's his wife, Lisa."

Lisa waved a hand. "Hi, Caleb, we've met before. I work at the office in the feed store."

"Good to see you, Lisa." He waved back.

Robert stopped unloading the scaffolding and came around to shake Caleb's hand. "I told Ava that I'd hang the lights on the eves, but she insisted I let her do it. You know what it's like to get caught in Ava's wake. When she sets her mind to something, you might as well surrender. It's going to happen."

Caleb looked back at her.

Ava notched up her chin and shot him a challenging stare. She knew where this was going, and she wanted to end it before it started. "Are you about to say something sexist, Sutton?"

"Is it sexist of me to want your pretty neck intact?"

She appreciated his concern, but she was more than capable of hanging lights on the house. "I hung the ones on the shelter all by myself. I can hang these lights on your house with half a dozen helpers."

"Half a dozen? I only count three."

"Mom and Dad are on the way, and they're bringing another one of our volunteers with them."

"It's my house, Miller." He growled. "I get a say in what goes on at my own house."

"If you'd decorated it yourself to begin with, we wouldn't be having this conversation."

Everyone looked at Caleb to see how he'd

respond, and she'd give him credit. He knew when to give up on an argument.

"All right." He snorted and threw his hands into the air. "Just don't fall."

"Gee, what novel advice. Why didn't I think of that?"

With a gentle tug on the string of lights she was holding, she climbed another rung up the ladder. Caleb's ranch house was sprawling, but it was only one story, so attaching the lights was easy-peasy.

She'd almost finished hanging the first strand when she noticed they had already added more strings. Glancing down, she saw Caleb had nudged Devon out of the way and he was now holding the ladder.

Ava met his gaze and laughed.

He winked at her conspiratorially and she had to admit, he was one handsome cowboy.

Her parents drove up just then with Skeeter, a skinny twenty-year-old woman who was studying to be a vet and volunteered at the shelter to get experience. There were more greetings as they all rolled up their sleeves and got to work. With the ten of them pitching in—Phil and Mort included—they had the decorating finished in no time.

"Who wants refreshments?" Caleb asked when

they'd packed the ladder and scaffolding back in Robert's truck. "I can't promise much, but I'm sure I can whip up something."

"Oh," Ava said. "We brought food with us. I promised a decorating party and I deliver."

Robert offered everyone cold drinks from his ice chest, while Ava and Lisa unloaded the food and took it into the house. Ava asked Phil to fire up the grill and within forty-five minutes they had a lunch spread of hamburgers, hot dogs, potato salad, deviled eggs, and baked beans spread out in Caleb's snazzy new kitchen.

"You never cease to amaze me." Caleb shook his head, grabbing a paper plate as she set out pickles and onion slices.

"Why's that?"

"For someone who doesn't like to plan ahead, you did a pretty darn good job of an impromptu get-together."

"Thank you for the compliment, Mr. Sutton. See? Spontaneity doesn't always equal scatter-brained."

"I never said it did."

"But you thought it."

"So you're a mind reader now? Something you picked up overseas?"

"I'll never tell." She returned his wink and stuck out her tongue.

"Watch out," he said. "I might consider that temptation."

She felt her cheeks flush, enjoying their flirtation. Still, she knew better than to rush into anything. They had agreed to take things slowly, which was the safe, intelligent approach since her future was up in the air, and by gosh, she was sticking to it.

Too bad she'd never taken the safe, intelligent road.

⸻

"What a fun morning," Marjorie said to Caleb as she walked over to the recycle bin carrying an assortment of paper plates and cups. "It reminds me of old times when your mother was still here, and you and Ava were dating in high school. Thank you for letting us take part."

"I should thank you." Caleb looked up from where he was cleaning the barbecue grill and met Marjorie's gaze head-on.

He hadn't expected today to turn out this way, but decorating had been a blast, thanks to Ava and her lively attitude. Plus, his house looked amazing. The place hadn't been decorated since his mother moved away, and it was great to see it all decked out again.

"I wish your mom and Chet could have been here with us," Marjorie said. "You should send her some pictures and let her see how pretty the place looks. She would love it."

"Good idea. I think I will."

Marjorie was right. His mother would love to see the house decorated and to know friends orchestrated the whole thing. Mom often teased him about being too introverted and too proud to ask for help. She was fond of saying, "No cowboy is an island, Caleb."

He searched for Ava and found her loading up her vehicle, and his heart skipped a beat. Spending time with her had him entertaining some pretty intense thoughts.

Marjorie picked up her glass of lemonade and perched on the picnic table next to the barbeque grill. Caleb kept his head down, scraping at the residue left from the hamburger meat and hot dogs.

The car's rear hatch door slammed closed and Caleb glanced up just in time to get a magnificent view of Ava's backside. The jeans fit her fanny as if tailor-made. Ava straightened, turned, and caught him staring.

A slow, knowing grin spread across her gorgeous face and she gave a little wave.

Dang it!

He went back to the grill.

Marjorie cleared her throat pointedly.

Caleb met her gaze.

Her eyes lit with a matchmaking light. She drew her jacket more tightly around her as the wind kicked up. "Ava tells me you two are dating again but are taking it slow."

Double dang it.

"That's the plan." It surprised Caleb that Ava had discussed their relationship with her mother, although he wasn't sure why that startled him. Ava and her mother got along well. No reason for her not to share what was going on in her life.

"Good idea," she said. "You want to make sure it'll stick this time before getting deeply involved."

Personally, he wasn't used to discussing his private life with people and he was uncomfortable discussing Ava behind her back.

"I'd hate to see you get hurt all over again."

"It'll be fine. We've discussed a long-distance relationship and we're hoping to make it work."

"But how? I mean honestly?"

That brought him up short.

Marjorie's gaze fixed on her daughter and she got a faraway look in her eyes. "I just don't know. She's currently out of a job and she doesn't seem in any hurry to find another one, but at heart she's a go-getter and there's nothing much to go get around here."

"That she is," Caleb murmured. He admired Ava's enterprising nature. Ironic that one of her best qualities was the same thing that had taken her away from him.

"I wonder if she'll ever satisfy her need to challenge herself and explore," Marjorie mused.

"You're saying I should abandon all hope for an eventual future with her?"

Marjorie locked eyes with Caleb. "I'm saying if you're waiting for her to change, you'll be waiting a long time."

Caleb didn't want to change her. He liked her just as she was, but was that enough?

You could always roam with her. She asked you to come along the first time. But that meant selling the ranch, giving up the one thing that had grounded him in his youth after his dad died. And what would he do with himself if he went with her? Ranching was all he knew.

And remodeling. You could buy houses and flip them.

"Ava is her own person," Marjorie mused. "She's always followed her own path in life. Even as a little girl, she was headstrong. I wanted her to wear dresses and frilly things. She insisted on jeans and sneakers."

"You ready to go, honeybunch?" Ted ambled from the house, settling his baseball cap on his head. "The dogs are gonna wonder where we've gotten off to."

"Yes." Marjorie got up. "I was just telling Caleb how much we appreciated him letting us help decorate his place. Now he's not the only house in Kringle without lights."

"That's overstating a bit." Ted chuckled and gave his wife a kiss on the cheek. "There's one or two other grinches in Kringle."

"I'm not a grinch," Caleb protested.

"No." Marjorie beamed. "Not anymore."

Thanks to go-getter Ava, he thought and closed the lid of the cleaned grill.

Ted laced his arm through his wife's and led her to their vehicle.

"Bye-bye, Caleb," Marjorie said with a jaunty

wave, as if she hadn't just stirred up a whirlwind of doubt inside him.

Thanks bunches, Marjorie. Drop a bomb and then just walk away.

Caleb blew out a deep breath and felt like cursing. He might not be the brightest cowpoke in the posse, but he knew a warning shot when he heard one. Ava's own mother worried that her daughter would break his heart again.

Ava was beautiful and fun, perky and smart. He knew why he kept falling in love with her.

Who you kidding, Sutton? You never fell out of love with her.

Stunned by the truth, he felt helpless as he wandered over to join Ava beside her parents' vehicle where they stood chatting. It was getting late and everyone was preparing to leave.

"We were just talking about the parade," Ava said, including him in the conversation. The Christmas parade was on Friday, and then Home for the Holidays was the day after.

"Are you all set for Home for the Holidays?" he asked.

"For what it's worth, we covered the entire town with posters." Ted grinned.

"Fingers crossed." Marjorie held up her crossed fingers.

"I bet a mob shows up to adopt. It's gotten a lot of publicity. We even got mentioned on the local TV affiliate." Ted slipped an arm around his wife's waist and drew her closer.

Caleb looked at Ava. "Are *you* set?"

"Yep."

He wanted to believe she was right, but he still worried about the small shelter's ability to handle a vast crowd. Ava might like to go with the flow, but he'd have felt better if she had a clear-cut plan.

"You'll get overrun," he mumbled.

She grinned. "Worrywart. We'll be fine. Several people have already stopped by to adopt early. Everything will be fine. Trust the universe for once, Caleb."

Caleb rolled his eyes.

"What? You've never heard the expression, 'Let go and let God'?"

"I'm thinking about the verse that goes, 'God helps those who help themselves.'"

Ava drew back her shoulders and thrust out her chin. "I am helping myself."

"Oh, really? Do you have signage directing people where to go? Are there extra volunteers scheduled? You need to organize your affairs. Things can go wrong."

"Maybe you need to trust me." Ava's smile faded. "I know what I'm doing, Caleb. Everything is going to be okay."

"She's got it under control," Ted soothed. "Ava's baking this cake; let's get out of her kitchen."

Okay, fine. None of the Millers worried about her lack of preparation. Why was he?

He knew if he kept talking he was going to say something he'd regret, so with a quick goodbye and thank yous to Ava and her family, he headed into the barn.

Ava was a spontaneous person, and when they'd been young, he liked that about her. She was so different from him, so full of life and joy. But now, years later, her spontaneity made him nervous.

He liked plans and organization. He felt uncomfortable when he didn't know how things were going to turn out.

Which was the problem with getting involved with Ava again. You never knew what was going to happen. Years ago, he'd had no clue that she was going to call off their engagement and leave town. He'd been blindsided.

Be fair. She asked you to go with her.

In the barn, he groomed one of the rescue horses he'd recently taken in. As much as he hated to admit it, he knew deep down the take-it-slow-long-distance approach they'd agreed on wouldn't work for him. If he spent too much time with Ava, he knew she'd break his heart again.

The smart thing to do was to call things off before they got tangled up again, before he got his heart shredded again. It didn't take a genius to know they would flop as a couple. They had fun, and deep down he knew he'd always care for her, but eventually their differences would drive them crazy. She would keep making spontaneous plans, and he would keep planning the fun right out of her.

"Life doesn't always work out as we'd like it to," he said to Charger.

The mare looked at him with soulful brown eyes. He, too, had been hurt because of someone who hadn't thought through the consequences of their actions. The gelding's previous owner hadn't found homes for his horses when his ranch failed. Instead, he'd just abandoned them, with no care for their future.

Sort of like Ava had done to Caleb all those years ago.

"You know what, Charger?"

The gelding nickered.

"I'm going to stop worrying and follow my heart whenever it leads me. I didn't do that ten years ago and look what it cost me. I'm taking a page from Ava's playbook and embracing adventure."

Charger whinnied and shook his head as if he didn't believe that for a second.

CHAPTER 9

CALEB COMMITTED to his plan to live in the moment, enjoying every second in Ava's company as if it were his last.

On Tuesday, the day after she and her crew showed up to decorate his house, Caleb invited her to the Christmas carnival. They held hands and walked through the crowds, savoring hot chocolate and Christmas cookies bought from the kiosk vendors on the town square. They played Christmas versions of midway games—Whac-an-Elf, Santa Skeeball, Reindeer Ring Toss.

Caleb was proud of himself when he won Ava a stuffed penguin from the ring toss, and when he handed it to her, her brilliant smile and warm hug had him feeling like a Kentucky Derby winner with a flower wreath around his neck.

They climbed on rides decorated for Christmas with gayly blinking twinkle lights—the Ferris wheel, carousel, bumper cars, and roller coaster. His heart expanded with Ava's screams of sheer delight. But his favorite ride by far was the Tunnel of Love, where they could smooch unseen from prying eyes.

Afterward, they ate funnel cakes and cotton candy, caramel apples and corn dogs. They danced at the line dance contest and came in last, laughing uproariously together in their last place trophy—a plastic statue of Santa Claus stuck in a chimney.

Caleb had so much fun, he wished the evening would never end, and when Ava invited him to go driving around to look at Christmas lights the following day, he immediately said yes. She left him wanting more at her doorstep with a quick kiss and a soft smile. Caleb floated home.

On Wednesday, after viewing the spectacular light show that Kringle put on for the entire month of December, they strolled the town square, hand in hand again, not caring at all that everyone knew they were together again. Then they got into Caleb's truck and drove around town, oohing and aahing over the houses decked out in lavish holiday decorations. This time, when Caleb left Ava at her door, the kiss that she bestowed on him was longer and deeper and by the end, his knees were so weak he could barely walk back to his truck.

Thursday, they went ice skating at the small indoor rink and skated to Christmas music until the place closed at nine. As they headed back to his truck in the parking lot, they heard a soft noise from underneath the truck. Ava put a restraining hand on his arm.

"Shh." She canted her head, the motion causing her hair to bounce against her shoulders. "Did you hear that?"

Caleb tilted his head too, straining to listen amidst the sounds of slamming car doors and purring engines.

The noise came again, a soft whimper.

Without warning, Ava dropped to her hands and knees on the pavement and peered underneath his truck. "Oh, Caleb, it's a little dog."

Hunkering down beside her, Caleb saw a small Chihuahua mix cowering against a tire.

The dog sure knew where to wait for rescue.

"We have to get him," she said. "We can't leave him out here alone in the cold and dark."

"We're taking him," Caleb said. "How are we going to catch him?"

It turned out not to be much of a problem. Ava had a packet of saltines in her purse and offered one to the little guy, who sidled closer and gobbled it up. When she extended her hand for him to smell, he sniffed enthusiastically and licked her palm.

She eased her fingers around him, and he only resisted for a second, his body stiffening and his eyes going wide, but she cooed to him and within a matter of minutes, he lay tucked into the back of his truck as they drove home.

It was after ten by the time they reached the shelter and confirmed that the dog was a he, thankfully neutered.

To Caleb's surprise, Marjorie was inside the shelter, sitting at her desk, inputting data on the computer. Juliet sat in her lap and when she caught sight of the dog in Ava's arms, she jumped down and ran across the room to greet them.

"Goodness, Mom," Ava said. "What are you doing out here so late?"

"Catching up on paperwork. I want to make sure we're ready for Saturday morning with a clean slate."

"We've got another intake." Ava held up the dog for Marjorie to see.

Juliet slapped her front feet on the floor, stuck her butt in the air, wriggled her tail for all she was worth, and barked enthusiastically at the other dog in a *come-play-with-me* yelp.

The dog in Ava's arms squirmed, his gaze targeted on Juliet. Both animals were fixed, so there was no reason not to let him play with Juliet. Ava set him on the ground, and he raced to Juliet. They danced around each other, playing and barking as if they'd reunited after a long time apart.

Caleb's gaze strayed to Ava. He knew firsthand what that kind of joy felt like.

"Looks like Juliet's found her Romeo," Marjorie laughed. "Let's check him for a chip. He seems in great shape. He's probably just wandered off from his owner. I'll go get the microchip wand."

Marjorie ambled to the door of the kennel and as soon as she opened it, the mass barking started.

Juliet and Romeo didn't even notice. They were sitting on the floor, facing each other, gazes locked.

"That is the most adorable thing I have ever seen," Ava said, taking out her phone to snap pictures. "This is going on the Kringle Kritters website. I've never seen such a case of insta-love."

Did you forget about us in freshman year? The minute he'd seen her in English class, he'd been head over heels and she'd told him later, when she'd laid eyes on him, she'd stopped breathing.

"I hope they get adopted together," Caleb said.

"Oh dang, I hadn't even thought that far ahead."

Marjorie returned with the microchip wand and she inspected Romeo. The little dog didn't have a chip. "Looks like you're staying with us, kiddo."

Caleb and Ava helped her with the intake process, and by eleven, they'd finished. Romeo had been fed and watered and was curled up in a kennel next to Juliet's. Marjorie walked back to the house with a flashlight, and parting instructions for them to lock up when they finished.

"Another fun-filled day," he murmured to Ava and drew her into his arms.

"It's been magical," she said. "I can't wait for tomorrow's parade. It's the highlight of Kringle's Christmas season." They held the parade annually one week before Christmas, so the date rotated. This year it was on Friday.

"I can't believe it's almost Christmas." He held her close and looked down into her beautiful face. "Are you ready?"

Ava laughed. "You know me. I'm a last-minute shopper."

"Spontaneous to the end."

"Yep. I bet you had all your shopping done by June."

"You'd be right." Except he hadn't yet settled on a gift for Ava. In June, he'd had little clue that things between them would develop so swiftly.

"And," she said. "I don't think I'd be off the mark if I guessed those gifts are already wrapped."

"Right again." He dipped his head.

She lifted her chin.

Their mouths met halfway.

It was a sizzling kiss filled with promise and Caleb could have gone on kissing her until he couldn't breathe, and he'd die a lucky man. But he had to get home and get some sleep. Tomorrow, he was riding in the parade with an equestrian group that rescued horses. After that, he'd spend the rest of the day with Ava, helping her prepare for Home for the Holidays on Saturday morning.

"Good night," he whispered and kissed her again.

"G'bye."

"So long."

"Au revoir."

"Parting is such sweet sorrow."

"*Romeo and Juliet.*"

"They are a pair."

"So are we."

"Star-crossed lovers."

"Good night."

"G'bye."

"We're stuck in a loop." She sighed.

He kissed her one last and then while he still had a feeble hold on his self-control, Caleb turned and sprinted for the door.

Ava settled into a lawn chair across the street from the veterinarian clinic on the parade route and glanced over at her parents.

Her folks were having a great time, visiting with friends and waving at people as they searched for empty spots to set up for parade viewing. Even though it was December, the weather was a balmy fifty-eight degrees at eight in the morning, so the parade had drawn a vast crowd.

After the parade was over, they would pack the local businesses. Exceptional news. Go pleasant weather! Just don't try to get into the Kringle Kafe.

Not that she could grab a bite with her folks at

the diner if she wanted to. She had to get back to the shelter. All the dogs needed fresh grooming for tomorrow's event and although she had volunteers, it was all hands on deck. Also, she needed to drop Romeo off at the clinic for Chloe to check him out and vaccinate him before he could be adopted. His infatuation with Juliet had held. This morning, when she'd let them out together, they'd romped for a full thirty minutes in the dog run.

Christmas music from the outdoor speakers enlivened everything, playing, "Have a Holly Jolly Christmas." Families lined the street, waving holiday-themed flags and banners. The scent of breakfast tacos wafted over from a food truck parked nearby. Ava inhaled, then closed her eyes and just savored the moment. She'd missed her hometown far more than she'd ever realized.

Her mother touched her arm to get her attention and Ava opened her eyes. "I thought I'd bake cookies when I get home for tomorrow's adoption event."

"Pets or people treats?"

"Both."

"What a lovely idea, Mom. Thank you! Are you making peanut butter cookies?"

Marjorie grinned and shook her head. "Nope. Pumpkin. Chloe shared a new pet recipe with me, and I avoided peanut butter in case someone has an allergy."

"That's really nice of you, Mom." Her mother was always thinking of others and planning nice things. "How in the world did you end up with a harum-scarum daughter like me?"

Marjorie laughed and patted Ava's hand. "I was very lucky, that's how."

"Even though I can be impulsive."

"Honey." Her mother patted Ava's cheek. "For every one of our perceived flaws, there's an equal strength on the flip side. Just because we have flaws doesn't make us bad. It makes us human."

"What's the positive side of impulsiveness?" Ava asked, feeling uncharacteristically broody.

"Oh, sweetheart! It's your sunny sense of wonder! When you were a child you'd always awake up with a bright beautiful smile on your face and ask, 'What adventure will I have today?' It was such a joy being your mother."

"Really? My constant quests for adventure didn't try your patience?"

"Oh, for sure! You wore me out. Many days, I just didn't have the energy to keep up with you."

"I wonder if that's how Caleb feels about me," she mused. "That I wear him out."

"Maybe." Her mother's eyes twinkled. "But I bet it's in a good way."

"Look," her dad said, pointing. "The floats are heading this way."

The floats appeared around the corner. Ava stood up with the rest of the crowd, waving and cheering for her friends in the parade. Funny how hardly anyone ever left Kringle. There were so many people she knew from high school taking part in the event, and she wanted to support them.

First came the floats for the local children's organizations. The youngsters were so cute and serious in their club uniforms. Next came the floats representing local businesses. Everyone had done a terrific job decorating. She waved hardest when the float for Chloe Anderson's vet clinic went by. Chloe was a real friend to the shelter, and she'd done a lot for Kringle Kritters over the years.

After the vet clinic float, there was one for the local bakery in the form of an oversized cake, one for the hometown grocer covered with giant fake fruits and vegetables, a flower-laden float for the florist, and a trailer covered with tools and gadgets for the hardware store. Huge megastores stores might have taken over most of the country, but thankfully a town like

Kringle was too small to attract them. In Kringle, most businesses were still small mom-and-pops.

Finally came the float everyone had been waiting for. Santa and Mrs. Claus waving enthusiastically to the crowd. The audience loved it, but their costumes looked like they would be uncomfortably hot. Ava gave her friends the credit they deserved. She imagined Zach and Suzannah could hardly wait to change out of those costumes. Even though a cold wave was coming through on Christmas Eve, the weather at the moment was picture perfect—unless you dressed like Santa and his wife.

After the float carrying Santa and Mrs. Claus went by, Caleb and the other horseback riders came through town. Although there were quite a few riders, Ava's attention riveted to Caleb. He looked so handsome in the saddle.

His eyes snagged hers and a massive smile crossed his face and he waved for all he was worth.

Ava's heart swooned. She could hardly wait until the parade was over and they could hang out together again.

The parade ended in a parking lot several blocks from the town square. Caleb had left his truck and horse trailer there, and after he loaded up Charger, he wandered back along the parade route searching the crowd for Ava.

But there were so many people he couldn't find her.

A happy mob had gathered around Zach and Suzannah as they climbed down from the float and headed over to the stage. Later in the day there would be a live band playing Christmas classics and he intended on bringing Ava here for the dance.

"Hey there, cowboy," a familiar voice said from behind him.

Caleb turned to find Ava standing there wearing blue jeans, a green-plaid long-sleeved shirt, and cowgirl boots. She'd braided her hair into two pigtails and she looked all of eighteen. His heart melted.

He loved her and that's all there was to it. Had loved her since he was fourteen years old. Come heck or high water, he would make this relationship work. He'd give her head and follow wherever she led. He was through with trying to control things. Overplanning had always been his Achille's heel, and it was time to let go of the reins and just let life take him on a grand adventure with her.

"Oh, look," she said, pointing at the stage. "Something important is happening over there."

Caleb turned to see Santa go down on one knee in front of Mrs. Claus.

"I think Zach's proposing to Suzannah!" Ava exclaimed.

Wow! He knew Zach and Suzannah had been seeing each other. Heck, everyone in town was talking about it, but he hadn't realized they were this serious.

Ava moved over to slip her arm around Caleb's waist as they watched their friend open a ring box and present it to Suzannah.

With tears in her eyes, Suzannah nodded, and then Zach was kissing her, and the crowd had surged forward.

Caleb stepped back, getting out of the way. He'd offer his congratulations later in private.

"You and Zach are close. Did you know about his?"

Caleb shook his head. "Nope. It's news to me."

"It's so sweet! I'm so happy for them both. Zach and Suzannah deserve all the happiness in the world." Ava gave a joyous sigh.

Caleb was about to ask Ava if she wanted to grab

a breakfast taco from the food truck when her cell phone buzzed.

She pulled it from her pocket and glanced at the screen, then looked up at Caleb. "Do you mind if I take this call? It's from one of the places I sent my resume out to."

"Go ahead." He forced a smile, but inside his gut twisted and a hollowed sensation dug a hole in his heart.

"Thanks." She answered the phone, plugging up her ear against the hubbub surrounding them.

Watching her, a sense of impending doom washed over Caleb.

Her expression went from eager to elated in two seconds flat. She mostly listened, nodding occasionally and answering "yes" many times. Then she finished with, "I'm looking forward to it. Thank you."

Caleb clenched his jaw, jammed his hands into his jean pockets, and braced himself for news he did not want to hear.

Ava ended the call and looked up at him. "I got the job if I want it."

He forced himself to smile and say, "That's wonderful news."

Anxiously, she bit her lip and shifted her weight. "There's just one problem."

"What's that?" he asked, trying to stay as nonchalant as possible.

"It's in Singapore and they need an answer by Monday."

CHAPTER 10

"MONDAY?"

"It's short notice and I'll have to cut my trip home short. That messes with the time we have together."

The news that Ava's job offer was in Singapore was a sharp kick in the teeth.

Staring at her, Caleb felt as if he were being pulled backward through a long, dark tunnel and his heart ripped out by the force.

"It's my dream job," Ava was saying, her face animated in a way he hadn't seen since she left for Paris a decade earlier.

She started listing off all the ways it was the opportunity of a lifetime, but she sounded tinny and far away and his mind couldn't fully process what she told him. The gist he gleaned—terrific pay, artistic freedom, liberal benefit package. The only thing that stuck in his mind and held was a single word.

Singapore.

"Caleb?"

"Huh?" He blinked at her.

She was standing there on the sidewalk, people leaving the parade weaving their way around them. "Did you hear me?"

He nodded, even though he hadn't. "Congratulations, Ava. I know this is an opportunity of a lifetime."

"It is." She nodded. "Singapore will be a bit more challenging on our relationship than if I'd gotten the jobs I'd applied for in Costa Rica and Canada but—"

"How long is that flight?" he asked. "Sixteen hours?"

She winced. "I'm not sure. Twentyish."

"So you really couldn't be any farther away from Kringle in the entire world."

"I know it sounds daunting—"

"No hopping on a plane for a quick weekend trip home."

"We'd have to—"

"Ava," he said. "Just stop."

She gulped visibly. "Stop what?"

"Trying to make this work. You are who you are. I have no right to ask you to be someone else for my convenience."

"Cabe, what are you saying?" She looked so distressed it was all he could do not to take her into his arms and tell her they would work things out.

"I'm saying we've had an amazing time this week. The best time I've had in a very long while, but—"

"I'll work on my flaws," she said. "I'll curb my impulsiveness. I'll—"

"You won't."

"Please give me a chance to prove myself. I—"

"Ava," he murmured her name.

"I will—"

"Ava, please let me say what I need to say."

She shut up and fixed her gaze on him, her eyes beseeching. "I'm listening."

"You're impulsiveness isn't the problem. Your ability to have spur-of-the-moment fun is part of who you are and it's why I love *you*. You are uniquely you, Ava. You don't make excuses. You grab life by throat and live it with gusto and I admire you so much for that. No, the problem isn't who you are. The problem is one of simple logistics. We can't build a life together while you are living ten thousand miles away. I was kidding myself to think it was possible."

Ava stared at him openmouthed. "You l-love me?"

"You know I do. There's been no one else for me, Ava, and I'll always have deep feelings for you. There's nothing like one's first love. There simply isn't. But it's time for me to stop hanging on to a dream. After seeing Zach ask Suzannah to marry him, it spurred me to face up to what I've been feeling for the last ten years. I've been lonely and waiting for you to wise up and come home to me. That was foolishness on my part. It's time for me to let you go. I want a wife and kids, the whole white-picket-fence fantasy, and you don't."

"I never said that, Caleb. When I was young, I wanted to find myself and I did. I learned who I was and what I wanted and after coming home and spending time with you, I know *you* are what I want."

He shook his head. "I'm in Kringle, Ava. Not

Singapore. You have your dreams and I have mine and I won't stand in your way."

Tears misted his eyes, but he'd be danged if he'd let her see it. He tugged his Stetson down low over his forehead and turned his face from her. "I wish for you only the best the world has to offer, Ava."

Then, while he still had his wits about him, Caleb jumped into his truck and drove away. He was halfway out of town before he realized he'd left his horse trailer behind.

━━━

Ava woke up Saturday morning with a heavy sense of dread sitting on her chest. It was ten minutes after six and still dark outside, but someone was banging on the shelter door and the dogs were going crazy. She'd barely slept last night, her mind in a turmoil over Caleb. She'd tossed and turned for hours, weighing her dilemma.

Quickly, she dressed in blue jeans, a Christmas sweater, work boots, and a hooded jacket and shuffled outside in the wan light of early dawn. She rounded the side of the house and headed for the shelter just a few feet away.

She stopped and gasped.

People were outside. Lots of people. Cars everywhere and more were pulling into the driveway.

Startled, she rushed up to the front porch of the shelter where an older man, holding one of her posters, stood banging on the door.

"The adoption event doesn't start until seven," she told him.

"I came early so I didn't miss out," he said, flapping the poster of Tiny the Great Dane in her face. "This is the dog I want."

"We open at seven," she reiterated, shivering in the cold bit of wind. The temperatures had plummeted since yesterday's pleasant weather for the parade.

"Tell that them." He jerked a thumb over his shoulder at the line of cars behind them. "It's cold out. Might even snow today or tomorrow, so you can't leave people running their engines."

The older gentleman was right. Ava hadn't expected this kind of response. She should have been more prepared. Feeling overwhelmed, she fumbled in her pocket for the front door key to the accompaniment of barking dogs.

Just as she was debating on how best to handle

the early morning crush, Caleb, Phil, and Mort came driving through the pasture on three ATVs. The cavalry had appeared. Gratitude swamped her as she tensed at Caleb's presence.

The three men parked their ATVs behind the shelter and strolled through the people collecting at the front door.

"How can we help?" Caleb asked, not a trace of emotion in his voice. He gave nothing away. She had no idea what he was feeling or why he'd shown up with his crew at the crack of dawn to rescue her.

Relief rushed through her hot and welcome. "You can get these folks settled in the outer office while I rouse Mom and Dad to pitch in."

Caleb nodded. "We're on it."

To the bottom of her heart, Ava appreciated his help, and she also appreciated him not gloating. She hurried back to the house and quickly woke her parents and texted the volunteers to see if they could come in earlier.

"How great that they can't wait to adopt," her mother said past a yawn as she shuffled to the coffeemaker in her slippers. "Your dad and I will be right with you."

Ava, too, was glad there were lots of interested people, but she'd never expected so many to show up all at once and so early. Now she knew why she'd been feeling dread since waking up. It wasn't just unhappiness about her situation with Caleb. It also was a deep fear Home for the Holidays might end in total disaster.

———

"You know you're an idiot, right?" Zach Delaney told Caleb after Caleb relayed what had happened between him and Ava the previous day. Caleb had been standing out in front of the shelter, still helping people form a straight line when Zach walked over.

"I'm not sure in what precise way I'm an idiot, but I figure you're about to tell me."

"You broke up with Ava, didn't you?"

Caleb blew out his breath, disgusted at himself for clinging so hard to his love for Ava. Why was it so difficult for him to let go? "Sort of, but how did you know that? Ava and I just talked it over yesterday."

Zach shrugged. "I could tell something was wrong the minute I showed up and saw that scowl on your face and you've been avoiding going inside."

"Maybe I'm scowling because this is such a madhouse. The crowd has been like this all morning. A stream of cars started driving past my house before dawn and I knew immediately what had happened and that Ava was unprepared for this, so Phil, Mort, and I came right over on the ATVs. I've been here directing traffic ever since."

"I don't think your foul mood has anything to do with the shelter and everything to do with Ava. Wanna talk about it?"

"I do not."

Caleb was glad his friend was here to help with the crowd, but his relationship with Ava was none of Zach's business. The reason it upset him *didn't* have to do with the shelter. Ava hadn't prepared for the onslaught of people, just like he'd warned her. Truthfully, though, he took no satisfaction in being right, but this event showed why he was smart to let her go.

They would never mesh. She loved to be spontaneous, while spontaneity stressed him out.

"You need to let her do things her own way," Zach said. "It might not be your way, but that's okay."

"This is advice comes from a man who has been engaged for less than twenty-four hours?"

"Maybe, but I've known for years that I loved Suzannah. Just took me some time to stop being an idiot and let her know. So take it from an ex-idiot, you need to be smart about this."

Except Caleb had already told Ava he loved her. In fact, it was his love for her that tore them apart. He loved her too much to tie her down.

Two more cars were pulling in, and Caleb directed them to the overflow parking with an orange baton.

"You need to think about what you want," Zach said.

"As if I haven't?"

"Don't always think about what's the smart thing to do. Suzannah and I both got caught up in that spider's web. Instead, think about what you *really* want."

Thing is, he wanted two conflicting things. Ava and his ranch, but he could not have both. Nor could he tell her about her father's cancer diagnosis and her parents' plan to close the shelter and move to town. It wasn't his place, and he'd promised Marjorie he'd keep quiet.

Last night, he'd known ending things with Ava was the right thing to do, but today he was miserable, and his feelings had nothing to do with the over-crowded shelter.

Truth was, Caleb had no idea how to fix it.

"Friend," Zach said, resting his arm on Caleb's shoulder. "I only know one thing. When you find a woman you love with all your heart and soul, you have to pull out all the stops to win her or you'll regret it for the rest of your life."

"Yes," Caleb said. "That all sounds good, but what do you do when it seems impossible?"

"In that case," Zach said. "You cowboy up and do the hard thing."

His friend's words hit him like a lightning bolt, and in that moment, Caleb knew the solution to his dilemma. Slapping Zach on the back, he said, "Thank you, man. Now I've gotta go."

———

It was five p.m. and Home for the Holidays was officially over. Ava, her parents, and all the volunteers had worked nonstop, Caleb and his hands included.

Exhausted, Ava slumped in the office chair beside her mom. Dad had gone into the house to feed Stephen King, Minnie Pearl, Oscar, Felix, and Cinderella their dinners.

"I can't believe we got all the cats and most of the dogs adopted out except for two." Ava yawned. "Someone even took poor old Waldo."

"It *is* a Christmas miracle," her mother said, sounding wistful. "The place hasn't been this empty since we started the shelter. And plenty of people would have adopted those last two if you'd allowed them to be separated."

Ava peered over at the Romeo and Juliet, who were curled up together on the sofa. "Mom, they adore each other. How could I split them up?"

"Most people aren't ready to take on two dogs at once. I appreciate that it's sad to adopt them out separately now that they've bonded, but they're dogs. They'll adjust."

"Maybe they won't," Ava said, toying with a pencil. "Maybe they'll always secretly pine for each other for the rest of their lives."

"Dogs don't have the same emotions that people do."

"How do you know?"

Her mother cleared her throat and sent Ava a pointed look. "This isn't about Romeo and Juliet. This is about you and Caleb."

She didn't even bother denying it. Instead, she got up and moved to the couch where both dogs curled up on her lap and gazed raptly into each other's eyes. Absentmindedly, she scratched them behind their ears and thought of Caleb.

Just then, as if she'd conjured him, the door to the shelter opened and Caleb walked in.

Immediately, Ava sat up straight, her gaze flying to meet his. "You're still here. I heard the ATVs start up and thought you'd gone."

He was holding his Stetson in his hands, looking uncomfortable. "I was about to head out. Phil and Mort have already gone back to the Leaping Long-horn. Just wanted to say congrats on clearing out the shelter."

Ava displaced the dogs and got up, her eyes clinging to his. Her stomach was tied in knots and she could barely breathe. "Thank you so much for everything. Honestly, we couldn't have done it without you."

"My pleasure." A quick smile appeared on his lips, and then it was gone.

Clearing her throat, she sent him a pleading expression. "Could we talk?"

He shook his head. "Ava, there's nothing to say."

Nothing? He wasn't even going to give them a chance to work through this. There had to be some kind of compromise. When two people loved each other...

"I've been selfish," she said.

"You haven't. You took care of yourself and that was wise. I admire you for it."

"I do too," her mother added from behind the desk.

"Caleb, if you just—"

"Ava," he said. "I have to go."

Putting his hat on his head, he turned and left her with a gaping wound where her heart used to be.

CHAPTER 11

"THERE'S something I have to tell you," her mother said. "And I don't want it to affect your decision about Singapore."

Ava turned back to her mother. What she hadn't told her mother was that earlier that day, after Caleb had come to her rescue, she'd made a very important decision regarding Singapore and had tested the job recruiter with her answer. That could wait.

"Mom?"

"Your father and I planned to wait until after Christmas to tell you, but I think you need the information now."

"And yet you don't want it to affect my decision?"

Her mother threw her hands in the air. "Okay,

all right, I know it will affect your decision, but I hate that it will. You need to make your choices for you, not me and your father."

"Mom," she repeated, feeling her eyes widen and her pulse speed up. "What *is* it?"

"Please don't panic—"

"Don't say that. Now I'm panicking."

Her mother got up, came over, took her by the hand, and led her to the couch. Ava's pulse went from a cantor to a gallop. "Mom?"

Marjorie eased between the doors and took Juliet into her lap. She motioned Ava to sit.

She did and gathered up Romeo, grateful to have something to hold on to. "What is it? Please tell me. I'm officially freaking out."

"Your father has cancer—"

That word. That horrible word. An icy blast froze the blood in her veins.

Her mother took her hand. "It's okay, okay. I'm botching this. It's skin cancer. Granted it could be a deadly skin cancer but it's not. They caught it early. It has like a ninety-nine percent cure rate when caught early. He's going to be fine."

Ava panted, her emotions knocked first one way and then another. Her father had cancer, but it was completely curable.

"Caleb knows—"

"You told him and not me?"

That hurt, but why should it? Caleb was closer to her parents than she was. She'd been globetrotting while he'd been here taking care of business. Love for him grew in her chest and swelled. He was such a good man and she kept brushing him aside for life on the road. Why? What was wrong with her?

"I'm sorry if we hurt you by withholding the information, but I'm telling you. Your father will have the mole taken out after the holidays and there won't even be any chemo. But—"

"But?" Ava echoed, clutching Romeo to her chest.

"His diagnosis has been a wake-up call. We're closing the shelter. We're renting a small house in town and we're putting this place up for sale."

"The shelter is your livelihood. You've run it since you first got married. It's been here thirty years. What will the town do for an animal shelter? You—"

"It's time for your father to get what he wants. The shelter was my dream and because he didn't have a strong preference as to what he did for a living and because he loved me, he did this for me. It's his turn now. He gets to plan the next thirty years."

"Oh, Mom! I don't know what to say."

"Say you're happy for us. We're looking forward to the next chapter of our lives. And thanks to you and your amazing photography and marketing skills, you've cleared out the shelter for us. It's the prime time to go. We only have to worry about finding a home for these two little guys now."

"I'll take them!" Ava said, still so overwhelmed by her mother's news that she couldn't think straight.

"To Singapore?"

The mention of Singapore stopped her in her tracks. Her mother's news changed *everything*. This was an earth-shattering moment, and Ava knew it was finally time to come home for good.

"Mom," she said. "I know just the person to adopt Romeo and Juliet."

⸻

Caleb didn't see Ava in the week leading up to Christmas. He'd made big plans for their future and he could only pray it was the right move. Until then, he'd have to wait to find out if she broke his heart again or if finally, they would get their happily ever after.

Question was, when to tell her what he'd done?

In his pocket was part of her gift. He'd picked it up in Dallas that morning.

It was late on Christmas Eve and he'd just gotten home from a holiday celebration with his mother and Chet and their friends. It did his heart good to see how happy his mother was with her new love. He'd told his mother about his plans for his future and with a fierce hug, she told him to go for what he wanted. That love was worth the risk.

Hope was in the crisp night air as he parked his truck in the garage and headed toward the house. He paused outside to admire the Christmas decorations that Ava and her crew had put up. He smiled. She brought such joy into his life. Nothing else mattered but his love for her. He had her Christmas present in his pocket and tomorrow, he would go over to the Millers and put everything on the line.

"Lost in thought, cowboy?"

Caleb whirled around and in the glow of the twinkle lights on his house, he could see Ava sitting on the front porch rocker in the dark, bundled up in a down coat, toboggan, scarf, and gloves. Stunned, he said, "What are you doing out here?"

"Waiting for you."

Heart pounding, he walked up the sidewalk toward her. "How long have you been here?"

She held up her phone and took out her earbuds. "Just finished *The Greatest Gift*. It's the novel *It's A Wonderful Life* is based on."

"How long is it?"

"About sixty pages."

"Why?"

"It's a great story."

"I mean why are you sitting here in the dark, in the cold, waiting on me when I might not have come home?"

"Please," she said. "You're a rancher. You never leave town for long."

"Why aren't you at home with your parents?"

"They're at a party."

"Why didn't you go?" He stepped up onto the porch.

"I wanted to see you." She stood up and stowed her cell phone and earbuds into her pocket.

"How did you get here? I don't see your car."

"I walked."

"The shortest distance through my pasture is over a mile."

"I wanted to surprise you."

"I'm certainly surprised."

"And I hoped to give you your Christmas present early. Just between you and me."

"Wait." He raised a hand. "I want to give you my present first, but let's get in out of the cold."

"Okay." She shivered.

He wanted to put his arm around her and draw her close, but he wasn't sure how she would react, so he didn't. Instead, he unlocked the front door and let her in. "Come sit. I'll start a fire in the fireplace. Make us some hot chocolate."

"Later," she said. "I can't wait anymore."

"All right."

They stood in the foyer looking at each other and for the first time since Ava decorated his house, Caleb realized someone had hung mistletoe from the ceiling above them. That was handy.

Her beautiful brown eyes were zeroed in on him. Breathless, she whispered, "Well?"

He reached inside his pocket and pulled out a palm-sized white box and passed it to her.

With trembling hands, she took the box and slowly opened it. Lifting the lid, she peeked inside. "It's a passport. Yours?"

He nodded.

"You haven't had a passport since you and your mom moved to the Leaping Longhorn when you were fourteen."

"Back then," he said. "I thought I was done with

traveling. Traveling reminded of my dad and remembering him was so painful that I shut down."

"And now?"

"Now," he said. "I want to go where you go. I want to be with you. I've got something else to show you."

"Oh, Caleb."

From his other pocket he took out a piece of paper and passed it to her. She read what was on it, her eyes growing even larger in her face. "You've put the ranch on the market!"

"I have. The day of your pet adoption event, I realized you were more important to me than anything else. And if Singapore was where you wanted to be, then that's where I would go. That's why I didn't stick around to talk to you that evening. I wanted to get to bed so I could call my real estate the next morning and get to work on an expedited passport."

"I-I don't know what to say," she stammered.

He searched her features, sudden terror gripping him. What if he'd made a huge miscalculation? What if distance and travel weren't the problem? What if she really didn't want to be with him whether in Kringle or Singapore?

Tears streamed down her cheeks.

"Ava." Fear constricted his throat and he struggled to push more words from his mouth. "What's wrong?"

"I turned down the Singapore job."

"For me?" His heart slammed hard against his chest and his hopes that had dipped rose again on fragile wings. Then another thought occurred to him. "Your parents told you about your dad's cancer diagnosis."

"They did, but I'd already turned down the job."

"For me?" he repeated. "You're willing to quit traveling for me?"

She handed him his passport and the real estate listing for his ranch. "You were willing to give up *everything* for me."

"I love you. I've always loved you, and I want to be with you. That's why I was willing to walk away from life as I've known it for the past fourteen years. You are the most important thing to me in the entire world. That's why my only concern is your happiness. Can you be happy in Kringle, Ava? Because I'm willing to go to the ends of the earth to be with you."

"I've got something to give you." She took two pieces of paper from her jacket and passed them to him.

He unfolded the papers, and when he recognized what they were, a smile overtook his face. "You adopted Romeo and Juliet."

"I couldn't let them be separated." Her eyes and voice were so soft.

"Oh, Ava."

"There's something else." She reached in the back pocket of her jeans for more papers.

He opened that up too. It was a bill of sale. All the breath left his body, every dream he'd dared dream was coming true. "You bought the shelter?"

"And my parents' house," she said. "I'm going to be your new neighbor."

"Are you sure this is what you want?"

"I've never been surer of anything in my life."

"But what about your wanderlust?"

"I've been there. I've done it. I accomplished that goal. Now I have other goals. I want to be here for my parents. I want to run the shelter. I'd forgotten how much I love animals and..."

He raised an eyebrow.

"I want to be with you. I want a life with you. I loved traveling and I wouldn't give anything for the adventures I had. It made me a more rounded person. But you know what?"

Caleb just shook his head, overwhelmed with love for her.

"Everywhere I went, the world over, villages and towns, cities and metroplexes, people would ask me what I was running from. Why I wasn't with my family and friends."

"What was your answer?"

"I told them I wasn't running from anything, that I was running *to* adventure."

"How did they respond?"

"Some people understood..." She shrugged, not caring the least what people thought about her. "Others said I was deceiving myself."

"And were you?"

"I guess maybe on some level I was running from an ordinary life."

"Wow," he said. "That's insightful."

"Ironic, isn't it? Now all I want is a nice, quiet, ordinary life in Kringle. I've learned the shiny new experience only lasts for so long and by flitting from place to place, hiding behind a camera, I never went deep. I stayed on the surface where it was nice and safe."

Was she being honest with herself? Did he dare hope she was home for good? Caleb worried about how much hope was in his heart. There was only one gift left to give her.

He took the little black box from his pocket and went down on one knee under the mistletoe.

———

Ava's body trembled and her heart filled with utmost joy.

"Ava Miller," he said. "This is the most spontaneous thing I've ever done. I just bought the ring this morning, having no idea whether you'd accept me or not."

"Caleb." His name came out in a rushed whisper.

"I've spent my entire life planning. I kept thinking if I planned carefully enough, I could control how things in my life went, but you've shown me that was wrong. I was trying too tight to hold on to you. The first time around, I was trying to keep you in a safe little bubble. I won't make that mistake again."

She'd made so many mistakes too. She should never have accepted his proposal the first time. She'd been madly in love with him, but she'd simply been too young. Now, she'd matured and grown. She'd seen the world, met many people, and no one had ever taken his place in her heart.

"Sure, it's good to make plans," he went on. "But it's also important to be flexible. I can't plan for every event, and it's wrong to try to control others. I need to be open to other ideas and to change."

"It's not a bad thing to plan," she said. "Home for the Holidays would have been a disaster if you hadn't shown up and organized the crowds."

"And if you hadn't spontaneously shown up to decorate my house, we wouldn't be under the mistletoe."

She knew he was right, and she couldn't help smiling. "So what you're saying is that we can depend on our individual strengths to build a life together."

He chuckled, the sound deep and reassuring. "Well, I wouldn't have said it that smoothly, but that's the general idea. I've been so worried about you leaving and breaking my heart again that I pushed you away. I realized at the pet adoption event how foolish I'd been."

"You're not foolish, and I love you so much." She was so happy to hear that he had changed his mind. She knew they were going to encounter obstacles in life. Everyone did. But she also knew that working together, they could overcome those obstacles.

"So what do you say? Will you marry me?"

Ava said softly, "It would be my greatest honor and joy to marry you, Caleb Sutton."

She put on his ring and he got to his feet and gathered her in his arms, and there, under the mistletoe they kissed for a very long time.

Ava hadn't just come home for the holidays. She'd finally come home for good and it was the most perfect Christmas surprise.

Dear Reader,

Readers are an author's lifeblood, and the stories couldn't happen without you. Thank you so much for reading. If you enjoyed *A Perfect Christmas Surprise,* I would so appreciate a review. You have no idea how much it means!

If you'd like to keep up with my latest releases, you can sign up for my newsletter @ https://loriwilde.com/subscribe/

To check out my other books, you can visit me on the web @ www.loriwilde.com.

Much love and light!

—Lori

ALSO BY LORI WILDE

KRINGLE, TEXAS

A Perfect Christmas Gift

A Perfect Christmas Wish

A Perfect Christmas Surprise

TEXAS RASCALS SERIES

Keegan

Matt

Nick

Kurt

Tucker

Kael

Truman

Dan

Rex

Clay

Jonah

ABOUT THE AUTHOR

Lori Wilde is the New York Times, USA Today and Publishers' Weekly bestselling author of 92 works of romantic fiction. She's a three time Romance Writers' of America RITA finalist and has four times been nominated for Romantic Times Readers' Choice Award. She has won numerous other awards as well.

Her books have been translated into 26 languages, with more than four million copies of her books sold worldwide.

Her breakout novel, *The First Love Cookie Club*, has been optioned for a TV movie.

Lori is a registered nurse with a BSN from Texas Christian University. She holds a certificate in forensics, and is also a certified yoga instructor.

A fifth generation Texan, Lori lives with her husband, Bill, in the Cutting Horse Capital of the World; where they run Epiphany Orchards, a writing/creativity retreat for the care and enrichment of the artistic soul.

Copyright © 2020 by Lori Wilde

All rights reserved.

No part of this book may be reproduced in any form or by any electronic or mechanical means, including information storage and retrieval systems, without written permission from the author, except for the use of brief quotations in a book review.

Made in the USA
Columbia, SC
06 December 2020

26577529R00114